T0132173

Sarah Woods
Is Unborderline

Monica Ashtyn Agius

BALBOA.
PRESS
A DIVISION OF HAY HOUSE

Balboa Press books may be ordered through booksellers or by contacting:

Balboa Press
A Division of Hay House
1663 Liberty Drive
Bloomington, IN 47403
www.balboapress.com
1 (877) 407-4847

Print information available on the last page.

ISBN: 978-1-5043-9583-0 (sc)
ISBN: 978-1-5043-9584-7 (hc)
ISBN: 978-1-5043-9626-4 (e)

Library of Congress Control Number: 2018900934

Balboa Press rev. date: 02/06/2018

Contents

Dedication

To those who feel they are living on the emotional edge and want to find a different way.

Introduction

Sarah Woods is Unborderline

"I am in love with someone."

I was sitting across from my friend, enjoying a drink after watching a show together, when I said the six words which were the catalyst for transforming my life.

"I'm in love with a man I saw presenting at a conference."

My best friend of over 20 years, Jamie, became concerned that I was being unfaithful to my husband and wanted to know all the details. But her concern for my marriage soon turned to concern for my mental health.

"I saw him give a presentation at a nutrition conference. He was attractive but not too attractive, and he was intelligent. I need to find a way to meet him, because I'm sure we are meant to be together, and he will fall in love with me too. The only problem is I googled him, and it looks like he is engaged."

"You know that's not normal right - to believe you are in love with someone you don't even know. I don't even know where to start, you need to talk about this one with your counsellor."

And that's how my friendship with Jamie went. The things I told her would often blow her away as she offered her support but struggled to understand the rationale behind my thought processes. She would then tell me that she couldn't even begin to understand how I got to 'that point' and that I needed to speak to my counsellor. The sad thing is that in this case, like many times before, I didn't realise that my way of thinking wasn't normal. This was how I lived, falling in love again and again and again, and obsessing about random people I had barely spoken with.

When I told my counsellor about the conversation I had with Jamie and asked for her opinion, she decided in an instant that my problems were beyond her capabilities as a therapist.

I had been receiving treatment from counsellors, psychologists and psychiatrists on and off for over 15 years, but they had only scratched the surface, helping me to manage day to day events without looking at why I was repetitively having the same kinds of problems with relationships and experiencing severe depression and anxiety.

I had been on an array of medication over the years which always helped to instantly lift my mood. The right medication could take me from being a zombie that walked through her days at university without making eye contact with others or talking to anyone, into a vibrant communicative person who seemed to have a bright future. And as I got older and became a mum they could transform me from a lump on the floor (that my children climbed over) who catatonically did the daily activities required for parenting and living, to a mum who was happy, energetic and enjoyed time with her kids and other parents. But while medication helped to lift my mood there were still a great deal of things going on that I struggled with, most of them to do with intimate relationships.

When my counsellor decided my problems were too big for her to help me manage I started to see a psychiatrist. It turned out I was behaving very much like a person with Borderline Personality Disorder (BPD), and while other psychiatrists may have given me a diagnosis of BPD straight away, my psychiatrist refused to put this label on me, and instead focussed on why I was behaving the way I did and helping me find ways to fix it.

BPD is a mental health condition where there are problems with interpersonal relationships, mood, self-image, and impulsive behaviours. BPD is diagnosed when a person shows at least five of the following nine characteristics across different situations:

1. frantic efforts to avoid real or imagined abandonment
2. a pattern of unstable and intense interpersonal relationships characterized by alternating between extremes of idealization and devaluation
3. identity disturbance: markedly and persistently unstable self-image or sense of self
4. impulsivity in at least two areas that are potentially self-damaging (e.g., spending, sex, substance abuse, reckless driving, binge eating)
5. recurrent suicidal behaviour, gestures, or threats, or self-mutilating behaviour
6. affective instability due to a marked reactivity of mood (e.g., intense episodic dysphoria, irritability, or anxiety usually lasting a few hours and only rarely more than a few days)
7. chronic feelings of emptiness
8. inappropriate, intense anger or difficulty controlling anger (e.g., frequent displays of temper, constant anger, recurrent physical fights)
9. transient, stress-related paranoid ideation or severe dissociative symptoms.

Looking at the diagnostic criteria for BPD I could see that I had all nine of the features of BPD: I had an intense fear of being abandoned by a partner and of experiencing the horrifying feelings of emptiness that came with it; I had eating disorders and body image problems for most of my teenage and adult life; my behaviours when it came to spending money were impulsive (I would suddenly decide I needed a new piece of jewellery or furniture and go out and buy one that day); when I was at my lowest point I would self-harm by burning my arms with a cigarette lighter; my mood could change from normal to chronically depressed in an instant because something didn't quite go as planned; and I expressed anger as a crying outburst or 'temper tantrum' sometimes throwing dangerous items. On top of that I also experienced depression, anxiety, and irrational thoughts – which is hardly surprising when someone's life is an utter mess.

Unlike schizophrenia and bipolar disorder which are due to changes in the way the brain works and can therefore be treated with medication, BPD is thought to be largely related to life experiences as a child which have shaped our understanding of the world and how we relate to others. In people with BPD there are often experiences of abandonment in childhood or adolescence, disrupted family life growing up, poor communication in the family, and sexual, physical, or emotional abuse. Medication is rarely helpful in treating BPD. However, the good news is that even though many people with BPD struggle for a long time, with the right treatment, many recover (some studies have shown that 80% of people stop meeting the criteria for BPD for periods as long as four years, and 50% of people recover completely). My road to recovery involved therapy which helped me to heal from past experiences, and change my perception of myself, others and the world. Of course, because having BPD causes so much distress, someone with BPD is also likely to experience stress, depression and anxiety. Therefore, antidepressants, antianxiety, and mood stabilising medication can help with the accompanying stresses BPD places on us (even though they won't fix the problem).

I was fortunate that I had learnt to manage most of the problems which I had with family, friends and work colleagues while I was in my early 20's, so by the time I came to see a psychiatrist most of my problems were related only to romantic relationships. With my high level of motivation to overcome my challenges and the progress I had made so far, my psychiatrist believed I had the intelligence and resilience to work through my issues and overcome BPD.

So, the hard work of undoing my past and building a new me, a new me who could relate better with others was about to begin. I was referred to a psychologist who specialised in Dialectical Behaviour Therapy (DBT), a form of therapy designed to help people change unhelpful ways of thinking and behaving while also accepting who they are. It was time to get real and dig deep. My therapy involved fortnightly sessions with my psychologist, reading every book I could get my hands on about self-awareness; and taking part in group therapy sessions with others who had similar problems. It was all about understanding why I thought and behaved the way I did, analysing my responses and reactions to situations, and finding healthier ways to respond. I needed to pull myself apart from the core to rebuild a more balanced and healthy person.

A lot of the work I did was based around the work by Dr Young and Dr Klosko on schemas. Schemas or 'lifetraps' are destructive patterns of thoughts and behaviour which start in early childhood. Our lifetraps become a part of us and control the way we think, feel, act, and relate to others. My schemas of fear of abandonment, emotional deprivation, and unrelenting standards (perfectionism), were making life a very hard place for me to exist because I continually gravitated toward situations which reinforced them. Living differently took a conscious effort and lots of hard work – and yet the lifetraps continued to creep in again and again in different ways because they were all I knew and what I felt most comfortable with.

I learnt a lot through my therapy process, and continue to learn every day. A big part of my growth happened as I began to understand new concepts and terms which I had never even heard of before. Understanding how these concepts related to my life became integral to raising my awareness of why I had certain thoughts, feelings, and reactions and to rebuilding a new emotionally healthy me.

Throughout this book I share the concepts which reshaped my life and helped me to:

- understand the person I was
- 'unborderline' myself
- and become the person I wanted to be.

Prologue

My story

I am Sarah Woods. From the outside my life looks normal, but the truth is I have lived a life tainted by BPD. While the doctors say complete recovery from BPD is a possibility I still have the memories of how BPD controlled my life and I still wear the physical scars as a constant reminder of the way I used to be. Therefore, I call myself 'Unborderline'.

This book isn't about my story as much as it's about the things I have learnt to help me heal from BPD, but because we like to know the ins and outs of each other's lives, here is a snippet of how I have spent my 38 years on this planet.

1981: I was the oldest born of two children to working-class loving parents in the suburbs of Melbourne, Australia. I had an average and non-eventful childhood with dogs as pets, attending catholic schools, spending school holidays camping in different locations across Victoria with my family, get-togethers with my cousins at my grandparent's place every Sunday after church, and as much sport as I was interested in (mostly netball).

1986: I started kindergarten. I excelled academically at primary school and right throughout high school. I was always a little shy and unsure about myself. I was never in the popular group at school but had no shortage of friends.

1995: I was 14 years old and in Year 9 at high school. My parents separated and for the first time in my life I felt like I couldn't find my smile. It was no longer commonplace for me to be bubbly, friendly and energetic. Instead I retreated into my shell, was quiet around my friends, and gave up participating in school activities that I had previously enjoyed like netball and mock trial.

1997: The all-girls high school I was attending became co-ed for Year 11 and 12. I found it challenging to interact with males and found I became quiet and self-conscious around them. I had my first taste of self-image problems, began to put on weight and developed an eating disorder.

1999: I turned 18! I started studying Primary Education at a large University where there were more than 100 people in my course. I felt like I was an invisible person in a large crowd and found it difficult to head to a place every day where I hardly knew anyone. I was miserable for the first half of the year until I became more familiar with the routines and developed some friendships. I also had my first serious boyfriend, Daniel, who I was with for 1.5 years.

2000: I changed to a much smaller University and began studying Nutrition. Being a smaller university, I developed some very close friendships and felt much more comfortable. About half way through my degree I began to become more consumed with body image problems and my eating disorder escalated, I once again became depressed and withdrew from my friends – preferring to spend breaks in the library alone instead of socialising.

2003: I was 21 and in my last year of University. I was extremely depressed and withdrawn. I saw a psychiatrist and he told me there was nothing he could do to help my mood. I was at a loss and felt desperate. The next morning while driving to university with all sorts of thoughts going through my head, I started to scream hysterically. I pulled my car over and continued screaming until an ambulance arrived (it must have been called by people who witnessed the event) and I was taken to hospital. This was a new beginning for me. I was put on antidepressants for the first time and started seeing a psychiatrist.

2004: I entered the workforce and working life suited me. I enjoyed going to work and catching up with friends or going to the gym in the evenings and on the weekends. I felt confident and I had my weight issues and body image problems under control.

2007: I was 26 years old and got married to a man I had known for three months. The first five years of our marriage were busy with pursuing our careers, having multiple miscarriages, having children (two boys who were both conceived through IVF), having a failed business, and frequent house moves.

2014: I was 33. I moved away from Melbourne to a beachside town with my husband and our children. Our marriage had been stale for about two years and my husband and I thought that moving closer to the beach and living a simpler lifestyle would be a nice new start. I left my fulltime job, family, friends and supports and we moved to a place where we knew no-one. After three months we decided to separate. I was now a single mum to two kids, with no job, and no family or friends nearby.

I started dating someone not long after my separation. I liked that he gave me so much more attention than my husband ever did - but soon that attention verged on becoming controlling. I was happy to be separated from my husband but I was now a single mum to two kids, with no job, no family or friends nearby, who was in an abusive relationship. Life was not good.

2016: This was a big year for me.

Early in the year I broke up with my boyfriend and for the first time in years I felt truly free. I started developing friendships with people locally, I got stuck into fitness - surfing, netball again, and pole dancing. I cautiously started dating again by meeting men through dating sites. I got to know many different men, broke a few hearts, and had my heart broken by those I chose to become involved with.

I started seeing a new psychiatrist and psychologist who focussed on why I seemed to have so much trouble in intimate relationships. Over the next few years I spent a lot of time with my psychologist and reading everything I could about self-development, living with mental illness, and healthy relationships. Most of what I share in this book are things I learnt from this period in my life.

I started working out of the home again, back as a dietician. I didn't love it but the money was good and I could leave my work at work. I also worked from home making wedding invitations – I loved this work as it allowed me to use my brain and be creative while not requiring me to interact with other people too much.

2017: I was 36 years old. After many failed 'relationships' I met my current partner, Josh. He had similar interests to me, lived close by, and was just as interested in finding a long-term partner as I was.

2018 (Now): My partner moved in and we started the work of becoming a family with my two kids who lived with us full-time and his two kids who lived with us on alternate weeks. On the relationship front it isn't always easy – sometimes it is very hard – but it feels like all the work I have done over the past four years is falling into place.

Chapter 1

Anxiety

1. *an uncomfortable feeling of nervousness or worry about something that is happening or might happen in the future*
2. *something that causes a feeling of fear and worry*
3. *eagerness to do something*
4. *a medical condition in which you always feel frightened and worried*

The word anxiety appears many times in this book, in almost every chapter in fact. Even though uncomfortable nervous feelings had been a part of my life for as long as I could remember I didn't realise what they were or realise that I was experiencing anxiety.

Anxiety for me is a feeling of unrest, of something that keeps popping up in my head, of needing to 'slow down' my thought processes, and of feeling like I need to get something out of my head but being unable to. While it is normal for everyone to have anxious feelings from time to time, some people can be diagnosed with anxiety as a mental health condition on its own, or it can be a symptom of another condition such as BPD. When you consider that people with BPD have problems with relationships, self-identity, problems managing their intense emotions, and are prone to participating in damaging impulsive behaviours it is hardly surprising that they experience anxious feelings. My anxiety is usually about one of two things: fear of being abandoned (related to my abandonment lifetrap) which is a big part of BPD; and feeling uncomfortable about 'not knowing'– not knowing what will happen... not knowing what someone thinks of me... finding the wait to 'find out' unbearable.

My first memories of anxiety are of when I had my first job at Time Zone (a video amusement centre for kids and families). On a few occasions when I would have to call in sick or to change a shift I would feel immensely nervous before hand, like I was going to be sick. I would make the phone call and it would go well with my manager being understanding and friendly about the situation but the nervous feeling would become a big bad lump in my chest and I would feel even worse after the phone call than I did before it. I could never quite work out why I felt that way but now I think it must have been that I was worried about what my manager would think of me. After replaying the conversation I had with my manager over and over in my mind, without feeling any better, I would always end up calling my best friend, Jamie, who helped me to see the situation rationally and calm down.

The truth is I grew up surrounded by anxiety and learnt that being anxious, especially about new situations and what people thought of me, was the norm.

As a child I would go to school friend's birthday party and when I came back there would be a heap of questions from my parents. Of course, there would be the usual questions like, 'Did you have fun?' and 'What games did you play?' But there were also questions about other people's responses, like, 'Did she like the present?' 'What did she say about the present?' 'Did anyone say anything about your new dress?' I was learning to be concerned about what others thought of me and to tune in to their responses and reactions to me.

I was also learning to worry and think the worst of situations. When my brother and I were little and would go to the beach with our cousins, the other children would have fun climbing on the rocks to look for crabs and other sea creatures with their parents watching from the distance, while we weren't allowed to join in unless our parents were by our side, because my mother was concerned that this was a dangerous activity and we may get hurt.

All parents have their own style of parenting and I know that mine were doing the best they could to show love, care, and protection for their children. It is interesting that the same parenting style can have a different effect on each child – while I developed anxiety and have strong memories of being parented in an anxious and overprotective way my brother doesn't share these problems or have the same memories. Do I experience anxiety because I was an oversensitive child – paying far more attention to the fine details of my parent's behaviour, moods and words than most other children would have? Was it because I was more obedient than my sibling and would listen to my parent's instructions – sitting to the side and watching other kids climb on rocks at the beach, while my brother was more inclined to sneak off and do it anyway? Would I have developed anxiety regardless of the environment I was raised in? Was my experience different than my brother because I was the first born? I will never know the answer to these questions, but I do know that for some reason I picked up on the well-intentioned concerns of my parents and grew up with them becoming a part of the way I also perceived the world.

I didn't realise that I had become conditioned to have 'anxious' thoughts until I was 21 years old. On this day I had a psychologist appointment to go to but I was worried about driving in the expected storm. I remember ringing my psychologist and telling her I couldn't come to the appointment because it was expected to storm and her response was to question where I got that crazy idea – why did I need to cancel the appointment because of a possible storm? That day I made a decision that fear and anxiety would stop then and there and I wouldn't let them be a part of my life anymore – I would create a new norm of behaviour.

And so I began living life with gusto... if something scared me I did it more! I did it until the fear went away – climbing on the rocks at the beach, going out when I hardly knew anyone, swimming in the ocean, competing in sporting events where people might 'watch me' and think I wasn't good enough – I fought against my anxiety as hard as I could to live a full, adventurous and fun life. But anxiety reared its head in other ways...

Not being able to let go of things and thinking about them again and again is called rumination and is a big part of anxiety. Just like the conversations with my manager (when I called in sick for work), I have always tended to repeat conversations over and over, analysing what was said and how it was said, wondering whether I should have said something a little differently and how that would have changed situations. There were times when my rumination drove me crazy and I wished I could silence the ongoing thoughts about everything and anything.

My anxiety was at its worst after my separation with my husband. My husband and I had been married for seven years and had only recently moved away from Melbourne to the coast to try to live a simpler life by the beach. With no connections on the coast the move meant leaving my full-time job, leaving my family and friends, and starting from scratch. As scary as that might sound I was excited about the opportunities it brought with it – a life by the beach, being a stay-at-home mum for the first time, and hopefully rekindling a marriage which had been beyond stale for over two years. Unfortunately, three months after the move my husband and I decided there was nothing to save and we had taken each other as far as we could in our lives together – we got each other to our dream location and lifestyle by the beach and that was as far as our journey would take us.

If being a single mum in a town where I knew nobody, with no source of income, and raising two kids virtually on my own wasn't stressful enough, I then started dating a man who I will call 'Grumpy Tradie'.

Grumpy Tradie was always upset or angry about something. Spending hours listening to him grumble about how stupid someone at work was or how the price of fuel is too high or how a loaf of bread isn't as big as it used to be was common place. I didn't mind supporting Grumpy Tradie as he talked through his 'hardships' but soon I became a hardship too and everything I did was cause for complaint or the silent treatment.

There were constantly things to worry and feel panicky about with Grumpy Tradie. Did I say the wrong thing? Why was he upset at me? How long before he breaks the silent treatment? When he finally breaks the silent treatment will he be nice to me or horrible to me? Being in that relationship caused me so much anxiety that my memories of that time in my life are of me being a jittering mess – sitting still but tapping my fingers repetitively on the table while staring into space; and of me being a lifeless mess curled up in the corner of my bedroom too exhausted from crying to cry anymore.

Even when I wasn't a jittery or lifeless mess my rumination was driving me crazy and it felt like there was a constant chatter in my head about things that had happened, conversations which had been had, and things that were coming up. There was so much uncertainty. At the time, the only thing which helped to silence the thoughts was antianxiety medication. I required such a high dose of medication to silence the thoughts and provide some peace that I became zombie-like as a side effect. To get through the day I needed a three-hour nap after lunch, and my care factor about anything was almost non-existent. It wasn't a great way to live but it's what I needed to do to get through a period in my life when the repetitive thoughts were unbearable. Eventually I realised that I needed to cut down my medication so that I could

5

function and to find other ways to manage the anxiety which then resurged.

Anxiety is such an uncomfortable feeling. Unlike depression which makes me feel like I am slowly coming to a grinding halt as the cogwheels become harder and harder to turn, anxiety keeps me awake, jittery, panicky, constantly worrying, moving constantly and with a feeling that I need to take action - to do anything to fix and stop the thoughts and unsettling feelings of 'not knowing'.

I eventually learnt some great strategies for managing my anxiety (meditation was a big one) and with the work I have done on myself my exposure to situations which cause me anxiety has drastically decreased (for example, I stopped dating men who treated me poorly). That's not to say I don't experience anxiety at all (even trivial things like waiting to hear from someone to lock in a date in my calendar can cause me to be anxious). However, having a word for that horrible feeling and understanding what it is, has gone a long way toward managing it.

Chapter 2

Obsessions and compulsions

At about the same time that I started seeing a psychologist during the last years of my marriage I noticed there were a large number of things about myself which I didn't understand and which were bothering me:

Why was it that while waiting at my kids' school (at either drop off or pick up time) did I feel the urge to pounce on my kids' teachers with something 'important' to discuss, even when there was nothing to discuss? I tried to control this by telling myself over and over as one of their teachers approached that I would just say, 'hi', but at the last minute I was always compelled to jump up and discuss something with them. This behaviour was driving me crazy and I could tell by the way the teachers avoided eye contact with me that it was driving them crazy too!

Why when drinking water from a drink bottle did I always need to take six mouthfuls and couldn't put my bottle down without doing so? If I went over I would need to start counting my mouthfuls again at number one, until I got back to having had six.

7

Why when encountering a new man of about my age did my mind immediately jump to thoughts of falling in love with him (despite being married)? And why was I compelled to find out everything I could about him via Google and Facebook?

Why once I was single did my obsession with finding a partner have me compulsively using dating sites - needing to check my profiles hourly rather than every so often. I knew this was unnecessary, excessive and probably a deterrent to anyone getting to know me, but I couldn't control the urges to keep checking.

When I started seeing a psychiatrist we realised I had Obsessive Compulsive disorder (OCD) which is a kind of anxiety disorder and often also occurs in people with BPD.

When people think about OCD they think about people who need to have their house or desk in perfect order, wash their hands excessively, or need to do things the same way every time. There is more to OCD than that. A simple explanation of OCD is excessive thoughts (obsessions) which lead to repetitive behaviour (compulsions).

In more detail, the obsession part of OCD is unwanted thoughts, urges or impulses which cause distress. The person tries to ignore, supress or neutralise these thoughts urges and impulses with some other thought or action. This is the compulsion part of OCD. While the person may not get any pleasure from carrying out the behaviour it helps to give some relief from the obsessive part of the disorder.

For example, with my obsession for dating sites, I was constantly thinking about finding a relationship and how miserable my life would be if I was forever single. Checking my dating profile gave me a sense of short-lived relief from those thoughts. While you might think that this behaviour makes sense because having an active online dating profile is likely to increase the chances of meeting someone, I could have had similar results by checking it once a day only. Checking every hour wasn't productive and it didn't feel good, it just gave temporary relief from the obsessive thoughts and anxious feelings. It was also very time consuming and made it hard for me to be productive at work, home, and in relationships with my kids, family and friends.

To make things more complicated, when my psychiatrist and I started looking at my diagnosis of OCD we realised that I had a less commonly known form of OCD called Pure Obsessional OCD or Pure O. This is when the obsessions are unwanted thoughts or mental images of committing an act which we consider harmful, violent, immoral or inappropriate.

Have you ever seen a person with crutches walking down the street and found yourself thinking, "Wouldn't it be funny if they fell over?" and then feeling shocked with yourself that you thought something so awful? Where does such a thought come from? This is a little of what it is like to have Pure O.

Pure O has given me repetitive brief thoughts of disgust toward people that I love and care for deeply.

Pure O has given me repetitive thoughts of wanting to kiss a man I used to work with even though I found him very unattractive.

Pure O has put images in my head of pushing over an elderly or disabled person so they fall to the ground.

Pure O has given me thoughts and impulses to snatch food from people's plates while they aren't looking.

Over the years Pure O has put other thoughts into my head which are too distressing to share.

Before I understood the diagnosis of Pure O I questioned why I would have such horrible thoughts given that I knew I was a good person and would never intentionally hurt or harm anyone. But that's the thing with Pure O - the thoughts are always of things which are so far removed from anything we would ever do which is why they are so disturbing and cause feelings of shame and disgust with ourselves.

My psychiatrist told me a few stories about the kinds of thoughts some of his patients with Pure O had experienced to reassure me that I wasn't alone in having these experiences.

Imagine being a new mum and having thoughts of sexually abusing your baby every time you change his nappy. My psychiatrist told me about this patient to help me feel less upset about an intrusive thought I was experiencing. This patient was so shocked and disgusted in herself because of the thoughts she was having. She tried everything she could to keep the thoughts away including changing her baby's nappy in different rooms of the house, changing it while talking on the phone as a form of distraction, singing songs while changing the nappy, and waiting for as long as she could until someone came over or her husband came home from work (so they could change the nappy instead).

Another story he told me was of a lady who had intrusive thoughts that her landlord (who was an absolutely lovely man) had raped her. Whenever he came over to collect the rent or do maintenance on the apartment she would be terrified of opening the door and letting him in because of the thoughts which kept popping into her head.

Imagine having thoughts like this pop into your head at random times. Imagine getting through life this way – having to ignore the thoughts of your mind. Before I understood that these thoughts were a part of a disorder (and didn't mean I was an evil human being) I often saw suicide as the only way out – because how do you live with that kind of evil going on in your own head? Fortunately finding out about Pure O and having confirmation from my psychiatrist that people with Pure O never act on the thoughts allowed me to continue.

Luckily for me the medication I am on to manage my anxiety has also helped to reduce my OCD and Pure O. I have also been able to develop some strategies for managing them when they do occur.

My strategies for managing Pure O thoughts

I have developed two strategies for managing Pure O thoughts which have helped immensely. To put these in place it was important that I understood and believed that the thoughts were not really a part of who I am but were due to a part of my brain circuitry that goes a little haywire from time to time.

Strategy 1: When an intrusive thought pops into my mind I separate myself from the thought by imagining that it is coming from an annoying parrot sitting on my shoulder. To stop the thought I tell the parrot to 'shut up'. I tell the parrot to 'shut up' every time the thought pops into my head and try not to give it any extra thought. This takes away some of the guilt related to having awful thoughts and minimises their impact on distressing me or interrupting what I am doing.

Strategy 2: For distressing thoughts that won't go away I imagine a comical version of the situation every time the thought pops up. For example, when the thought of kissing the man at work who I found unattractive popped up I imagined us both as cartoon characters, with exaggerated features getting married. Me with a big boofy wedding dress, and him in a suit which was too small for his large body and a tie that ends just past his chest. Comical images are often enough to break the thoughts and have me giggling instead of feeling distressed.

Chapter 3

Abandonment

On my first day of school at four and a half years old, I had my first taste of abandonment. The impact of that morning shaped my future and the way I formed intimate relationships.

As with many children in the 1980's I grew up in a household where my mum was the primary care giver and didn't work out of the home. Other than when my mum was in hospital giving birth to my younger brother and I was looked after by my dad and grandparents, I don't recall being looked after by anyone but my mum.

So, turning up at school in February 1986 with my mum and dad, and knowing that my mum would be leaving my side for the first time was frightening. Not only was I scared of being left alone, but I was acutely aware that I didn't know how I would respond to being left alone, so I was afraid of what my response might be too. I remember being uneasy about my parents leaving me, and clinging to my mum – wanting her to stay with me in this unsure, unfamiliar environment.

The bell had gone and other children were starting to gather around the classrooms, and I was still a little upset but preparing to leave my mum's side. My mum had an unsure look about her as she suggested I go to the toilet and then come out and give her a big hug goodbye before I made my way to the classroom.

While I was in the bathroom I tried to compose myself. I wiped away my tears with the back of my hands, one hand for each eye, and rubbed my wet hands on the back of my green school uniform to dry them. I took a deep breath, and looking at my teary red and wet face in the mirror told myself that I was going to be strong, I was going to be brave, and I was going to make my mum proud by giving her a hug goodbye and walking into the classroom without tears in my eyes.

But of course, my parents did what many parents did in that day when a child was being clingy at school drop offs - they left without saying goodbye. When I walked out of the toilet, my mum and dad were nowhere to be seen.

The only other thing I remember about that morning is that while I was crying hysterically at the back of the classroom with a little boy, Patrick (who I am still in contact with via Facebook), the teacher looked over at me and said, "It's only a day at school, no-one is going to hurt you. I don't know why you are so upset." I didn't know how to articulate that I wasn't upset about being at school, or even about missing my mum. I was upset because she left me - she abandoned me. And with that I cried louder and harder.

Fast-forward seven years, and I hardly even flinched when on my first day of high school my mum dropped me off 30 minutes before the school opened, because she needed to get to work. As an 11-year-old, I waited in the quadrangle with one other student who had arrived early, until teachers and students (many of them with their parents by their sides until the bell went) started to arrive. "I was fine. I was strong, tough and independent," I thought to myself as I bravely told my mum that it was fine for her to go. I didn't realise I was upset about being left alone until years later when I understood that my acceptance of the situation was more than a sign that I was tough and strong, sadly it was an acceptance that I needed to be able to do things on my own because I had learnt that there was always a risk of being abandoned. Being acutely aware of the risk of abandonment was a part of my life - something that

13

would shape the ways I formed intimate relationships with others, until I had the knowledge to do something about it.

The feeling of being abandoned didn't rear its head again for me until many years later and it was much later again before I knew what that horrible feeling was and could give it a name.

After my marriage broke up and I started dating I became all too familiar with the gut wrenching feeling of abandonment. The typical story was that I would go on a date or two with someone and have a wonderful time, and he would promise me that we would see each other again soon. At first he would contact me regularly but as soon as I made it clear that I was looking for a relationship and wasn't available for quick and easy sex, the days between contact got longer. With the gap between contact increasing I would start to feel that I wouldn't hear from him again and I would feel a darkness overwhelm me and eventually it would plunge me within myself, into a deep depression. When it became clear that I wasn't going to hear from or see this person again I would feel like I had been punched in the chest with a sledge hammer. The pain was unbearable and all I wanted to do was lock myself away and cry like a child. At the time I didn't understand how someone I had been on a few dates with could have me so depressed.

It didn't just happen with men I had only been on a few dates with, the same thing happened with men who I had dated for several months, except the difference was that the relationship would go along smoothly, and just as we reached a milestone, like me spending the night at his place or him introducing me to someone as his girlfriend I would reach a level of calm, just in time for him to retreat, leave bigger gaps between contact, and eventually end the relationship. Again, the darkness would engulf me, and I would begin to become depressed, up until the final blow when the relationship officially ended and I would become an utter blubbering and crying mess for days.

It was one particular relationship ending in this way, through no fault of my own, that helped me to discover what that horrible dark feeling was – that it was the feeling of being abandoned.

I had been dating a man I will call 'Smug Lawyer' for three months. Smug Lawyer had only recently separated from his wife so I was realistic that things could only progress at a slow pace, although they seemed to be progressing well. We got along well, had fun, and were able to speak about all sorts of deep and meaningful things. At about the three months mark we became 'friends' on social media. And while I saw this as big step in the right direction I think it was a sign for him that things were progressing in a direction he didn't feel comfortable with. Smug Lawyer phoned me one morning, as I was preparing a romantic picnic lunch on the beach for us, to tell me that he couldn't come over, and that he needed to end our relationship – I'll get to the reason why he needed to end the relationship in a little while, but he needed to end it, and he was clear that it wasn't because of anything I had done or not done. All I could think was that I had been nothing but a patient, kind, caring girlfriend and now I would never see him again. Of course, I went from a happy woman about to have a romantic picnic lunch to an utter crying mess. I had two sick days from work, was unable to look after my children properly, and cried until there were no tears left.

When the tears finally started to dry up I was left with intense anger at him for 'doing this to me' and the feelings I had reminded me of feelings I had experienced once before – I felt the same way as I did when one of my closest friends told me she had decided to move interstate. I had developed a close friendship with one of the mums, Laura, from a mother's group I was part of when I had my first baby. We both had little boys of the same age, lived around the corner from each other, and then both turned out to be pregnant with our second children at the same time

15

Laura was younger than me but so much wiser. I learnt so much about being a domesticated housewife and mother by spending time at her place, and watching her cook, clean, and wipe up, all while interacting with her kids and with a smile on her face, before she sat down for a glass of wine. She taught me to enjoy the role of being a mum, and in many ways, she was also a motherly figure to me. When Laura told me she was moving away I was intensely upset and angry at her. I knew I had no reason to feel angry, but I did, and I didn't understand why. I was so angry at her that I couldn't organise a farewell, buy her a going away gift, or even say a proper goodbye. And I couldn't stay in contact with her, because it was too painful. My angry feelings at Laura bothered me for a long time because I couldn't understand why I felt that way.

After the break-up with Smug Lawyer I realised what the feeling was, and why I felt so angry. The word ABANDONED came to me, and I realised that I was angry at Laura and Smug Lawyer in just the same way, because subconsciously I felt they had abandoned me.

It was then that I pieced things together and realised that the horrible darkness that I felt when dating situations didn't go well was a feeling of abandonment. That me crying for days like a little girl, was the same as me crying on my first day of kindergarten - not understanding what I had done wrong and how my mum could leave me. These strong feelings of abandonment, the flood of emotions which they cause, and then the inappropriate and intense feelings of anger are all features of BPD.

Back to Smug Lawyer and the reason why he needed to end our relationship. I will need to start right at the beginning to when he told me on our first date that he had been separated from his wife for three months. At the time I thought, "Wow, that's not long" - I was looking for someone who was interested in developing a committed stable relationship and I wasn't quite sure that this would be possible for a man who had only been separated for such a short period of time. But, as he seemed nice and said all the right things to reassure me that his marriage was definitely over and he was ready to move on I decided to give it a go. Then, when we had been dating for about three weeks it came up in conversation that he had actually only been separated for two weeks when we had met. Yes, you read that right, two weeks! I knew there was no way that someone who had been separated for such a short period of time would be available to develop a committed relationship, but as I was already invested, I continued to spend time with him. When he broke up with me he told me that he needed to end things as it was getting messy for him, as he had promised his wife (who was devastated by his decision to end their marriage) that he wouldn't date anyone for six months, and if she were to find out about us she would make it difficult for him to spend time with his daughter. I had been dating someone who wasn't available to me – I had been setting myself up for being abandoned.

Remember how I said in the introduction that our lifetraps like to prove themselves right and find a way to make themselves a reality? Well being abandoned was becoming a real reality for me as I continued to date men who were unavailable for all sorts of reasons – some obvious (like living three hours away or still being committed to their wife) and others not so obvious (like having their own emotional issues which stopped them from allowing people into their lives).

When I finally realised that I was setting myself up for abandonment I made a choice to be fussier about who I dated or got involved with. Because I was largely meeting people on dating sites it was relatively easy to weed some of the unavailable men out of the equation before I became 'attached'.

If they lived out of my area how was it really going to work once we wanted to take the relationship further? I couldn't risk the high chance of abandonment so they got the flick before I even met them.

Single for less than six months? How could they possibly be open to developing a committed long-term relationship? I couldn't afford to give them a chance either.

If on the first date they made a point of telling me how busy their life was, or talked constantly about their ex-wife – gone. They were too risky.

It might sound like I was making dating and finding a great man very difficult. On the contrary I had decided I wouldn't waste my time on men who were a high risk for me. Abandonment was too painful and too dangerous for my wellbeing – I couldn't afford to date someone who had high stakes of becoming unavailable.

Understanding my lifetrap meant that I could see the impact abandonment had in my life and I could make a decision to stay away from men who were unavailable and likely to abandon me. This knowledge allowed me to make changes to put abandonment in my past and to take back the control which I had lost all those years ago as a four-and-a-half-year-old girl on her first day of school.

Chapter 4

Triggers

If there is one thing my kids do which makes me furious it is stepping on the back of my shoes - usually thongs (flip flops) - while we are walking together. Over the years my kids have become accustomed to the fact that this makes me furious and will have me turning around with fire in my eyes and snapping at them to not do it again!

It took me a while to realise that when my kids step on the back of my shoes it annoys me because it brings back a memory of something which happened when I was on a holiday with Grumpy Tradie. I have already mentioned how Grumpy Tradie had the ability to twist any innocent comment, reaction, or event into a drama punishable with verbal abuse, silent treatment and nastiness. While we were on this holiday though, things were good. Grumpy Tradie and I were having one of those highs which is common in relationships where an abuse cycle exists - when things are good they are great, but horrible times are never far away.

The incident happened when we were walking to breakfast from our hotel room and I was wearing the only pair of shoes I had brought with me - my thongs. I vividly remember that just as I stepped into the elevator Grumpy Tradie stood on the back of my shoe so hard that the straps of my shoe ripped out from the base (to this day I don't know whether he did this on purpose or if it was an accident). With a broken shoe and a sore foot I wasn't feeling too great, but I felt as though I couldn't get annoyed, upset or complain or it would turn into another big fight. I shuffled around in my broken shoe for the next day and neither of us said a word about it.

So when my kids step on the back of my shoe the memory of that time in my life is reignited and I become unreasonably angry quite quickly. To be honest my extreme reaction shocked me the first few times it happened as I wasn't aware of triggers and that the anger was coming from being reminded of being in an abusive relationship. Over the years, as I have learnt more about triggers, I have become better at controlling my behaviour when things like this happen. Now, when one of my kids stands on the back of my shoe I take a deep breath before turning around and saying, "You know how much I hate it when that happens. Be more careful please." I do my best to control my anger and they also remember how violently I used to react and do their best not to step on the back of my shoe again.

Triggers are defined as something that causes someone to feel upset, frightened or anxious because they are made to remember something negative which has happened in their past. Triggers are common in people who have BPD because many of them have had traumatic experiences in their childhood and in relationships. A smell, sight, sound, thought, feeling, or situation can bring up memories of the traumatic event and even feel like they are reliving it, causing intense emotional reactions as well as physical reactions such as raised heart rate, sweating, and increased muscle tension.

The most common triggers in BPD are related to relationships. Many people with BPD experience intense feelings of fear and anger in relationship situations which make them feel rejected, criticized or abandoned. This can cause them to act impulsively, self-harm, and even experience suicidal thoughts. I have behaved impulsively and irrationally when feeling that an intimate relationship is at risk of ending, and experienced feelings of despair and thoughts of suicide when the ending has happened. I have also seen the impact that triggers can have in everyday events in intimate relationships.

Triggers are a huge cause of conflict and problems in intimate relationships. One person will say something or behave in a certain way and the reaction from the other person will seem out of proportion (because they have been triggered). Their reaction isn't due to what the other person has done, but is due to something which has happened to them in their past. I have been guilty of getting extremely upset or angry at someone because something they have done has brought up an emotional memory from my past. Because triggers bring up such strong emotions it can be hard for me to work out whether it's reasonable for me to feel the way I do based on what the other person did, or if the way I am feeling is due to my trigger. I have found that taking the time to think the situation through before reacting is worth it and is much better than getting angry at someone because of what someone else has done to me previously.

I was triggered by my partner early on in our relationship when he said to me, "I hope you aren't messing with me." We had just started to spend more time together and we were at the point where we were both starting to let our guards down and realise that perhaps this 'thing' could actually become something bigger.

What he was telling me when he made that statement was that he was vulnerable and didn't want to get his feelings hurt. What I heard was a line I had heard many times before in a variety of forms from Grumpy Tradie, throughout our entire relationship, "Is this a joke?" "Has someone put you up to dating me?" "Are you messing with my head?" I spent a whole year with a man who needed constant reassurance that I cared for him and then could snap at me and ignore me for days because I didn't reassure him enough or in quite the way that he needed. Hearing, "I hope you aren't messing with me", triggered me into feeling I was trapped in a relationship like the one with Grumpy Tradie again, and as a result I felt an instant surge of anger.

Luckily I knew about triggers because it would have been very easy for me to respond to my emotions at that point in time and withdraw or get angry at Josh. Instead, I recognised that as angry as I was feeling, it wasn't really him that I was angry at, and I tried to look at the situation rationally. Here was a man who was sharing with me, in the only way he knew how, that he had been hurt in relationships before and was concerned about getting hurt again. I took a deep breath, stayed calm and said, "I know what it is like to be scared of getting hurt - no I'm not messing with you - I really like you and hope this can progress."

Having experienced abandonment many times throughout my life, anything which signals that abandonment is on the way is a huge trigger for me in relationships. I begin to feel anxious and that heavy dark feeling begins to sit over me. I need to be exceptionally careful in relationships to not assume someone is going to abandon me and then get angry at them because of my feelings.

A couple of months into our relationship Josh and I were spending the day at my house running around after the kids. I needed to get out for a little while to take my youngest son to a friend's house and while I was gone he was working on fixing my older son's skateboard. It had been a big day, and Josh was going over and beyond to help me at home and with my kids that day - no-one could blame him if he was exhausted and fed up - but if he was he didn't show it, he just kept getting on with the jobs that he had decided to help me with. But when I got home from dropping my son off, Josh wasn't there - there was no note, and my son wasn't sure where he had gone. I immediately felt fear that it was all too much for him and he had decided to just leave. This was triggering my fear of being abandoned.

I told myself to stay calm and that he had probably just gone to get something he needed for the skateboard, but as five minutes passed, and then 10, and soon 15 and he still hadn't returned I started to feel that horrible dark pit draw me in. As calm as I tried to stay my son even noticed that something was upsetting me, "What's wrong mum?" he asked, "You look like you are about to cry."

Of course Josh returned not long after, and he had only gone up the road to the bike shop to see if he could buy what he needed to fix the skateboard. When he walked in the door he didn't know what hit him! I immediately ran over to him, gave him a big hug and started to cry.

Imagine if I didn't realise that the horrible extreme feelings I had were due to my past and instead blamed my partner for upsetting me. Imagine if I had phoned him, angry that he left without telling me where he was going, or sent him an angry text, or yelled at him when he came in the door. How inappropriate would that have been? What would have happened to our relationship if this was the way I behaved? People with BPD find themselves in situations like this all the time resulting in constant fighting and the breakdown of relationships. This is why it is so important for us to acknowledge our triggers and monitor the way we behave when we are affected by them.

When it comes to relationship development it is also a great thing to be able to let the other person know what our triggers are, not so they tip toe around us but so they can be aware of the little things they can do to help. My extreme response to the 'skateboard fixing disappearance' was the perfect opportunity for me to share with my partner the fears I have around abandonment and how scary it is for me.

A few weeks after the incident Josh showed the ultimate gesture of understanding and caring for me and my emotional needs. It was a Saturday night and we were planning a Sunday sleep in. Before we went to sleep he said to me, "Now, if I wake up earlier than you tomorrow morning I might go to the shops quickly and grab the paper and a few things for breakfast. I will be back, ok. I love you." My partner had realised how worried and upset I would have become if I were to wake up and find he wasn't in bed beside me. His understanding of one of the things I struggle with and the willingness to help minimise any suffering for me was so appreciated.

Things that help me manage my triggers

- I did the work to find out what kinds of things triggered me. I looked at common things that brought up strong emotions for me and how they related to my past.
- When I feel angry, upset, or have other strong emotions in a relationship I think about whether this is about what just happened or because of a past experience.
- I remind myself that it isn't fair to get angry at someone for something which was done to me by another person.
- Before reacting to my triggers I try to take a deep breath (or five deep breaths).
- I try to be brave and share my triggers with my partner so they understand what I experience and why.
- I remind myself that other people have triggers too. I consider what I may be doing to 'trigger' the important people in my life and cause conflict in my relationships.

Chapter 5

Fear of abandonment

The incident with my partner disappearing to get a piece to fix my son's skateboard may have revealed to you something which took me a long time to realise - not only have I suffered from being abandoned, but as a result I started to suffer from the fear of being abandoned.

When something happens repetitively we begin to expect that it will happen to us again and again and again. I was so accustomed to being abandoned in relationships that I looked for signs of it wherever I could.

The problem is that reading into everyday situations as a sign you are going to be abandoned and responding to them in that way really does increase the risk that the other person is going to think you are a bit too much hard work to have a relationship with and leave - and how can you interpret that as anything but being abandoned again?

Abandonment is one of the lifetraps described in the book, "Reinventing your life", and is very common in people BPD. Fear of abandonment is the feeling that the people we love will leave and we will end up alone forever. Because of this fear people with BPD may cling to those who are close to them, or get upset or very angry about normal separations.

Like many people with BPD my fear of being abandoned had me doing all sorts of crazy things in relationships and living with heightened anxiety. But what was I actually scared of? It took me a while to realise I was scared of the 'empty' feeling that comes when I am single or feel no hope at finding a partner. Chronic feelings of emptiness are one of the traits of people who have BPD. I would do anything to avoid the empty feeling and knowing that it was looming when a relationship was ending was terrifying for me.

The first time I experienced feeling 'empty' was when I was 15yo and in Year 10 at school. I remember lying in bed feeling absolutely miserable without understanding why.

Throughout my high school years, I was known by my friends to be 'boy crazy'. There was always one, two or three boys that I was interested in and developed a crazy infatuation for. It was rare for any of these crushes to develop into anything more than an acquaintance that left me feeling giggly and girly and spending hours upon hours daydreaming about – but my crazy endeavours to be noticed by these boys used to have my friends in stitches (like the time I sent an anonymous present in the post to one of them or the time I stayed home from school so I could time it to walk past their bus stop at just the time they got off the school bus only to say nothing more than, 'hello'). No-one quite understood why I was so 'boy crazy'. If I knew then what I know now, I would have been able to tell my friends that the hope of a relationship and the energy I spent day dreaming about boys saved me from feeling empty inside.

Back to the first time I felt emptiness… it took me a while to realise that I was feeling miserable that day because I was just about to lose contact with several of the boys I had a crush on – my neighbour (the one who I had stalked at the bus stop) was moving to a new house, a boy who my brother did AFL with was leaving the team and I would no longer see him at training drop-offs and pick-ups, and another of my crushes was moving interstate. This was before the days of mobile phones where you could send a casual text to keep in contact with someone, and way before Facebook where you could become friends via social media or at least check on their profiles occasionally to feel a sense of connection. Back then when you lost contact with an acquaintance it was pretty much over unless you bumped into them by chance.

The feeling of emptiness and misery I experienced that day verged on depression and I found it incredibly hard to manage as I had never felt anything like it before. Fortunately, the feeling was alleviated quite quickly – well, as soon as I found someone else to develop a crush on! Little did I know that I was starting a pattern of developing relationships to keep away the empty feeling, and by doing everything I could to avoid the empty feeling I was fuelling a fear of abandonment.

Unfortunately, after my marriage ended the fear of abandonment and of facing that empty feeling was part and parcel of dating.

This is a good time to share a story about a man I dated for a short time who had his own issues around being in a committed relationship. Let's call him 'Unavailable Teacher'. Unavailable Teacher appeared rather unavailable from our first date when he told me with pride how busy his life was with work, university, fitness, and a multitude of his daughter's activities to be involved with. I walked away from our first date thinking, "Wow, he is really nice, but he has no time for a relationship, his life is way too full already." First instincts are a very powerful thing! He had very little time and led a busy life, as many of us do, but more importantly he had no plans to do anything about that. As much as he wanted a relationship and felt that it was the right time for him to meet someone, he feared relationships and didn't want to let anyone into his life or emotional space. Without realising it himself, he was telling me loud and clear on that first date that he wasn't 'available' for a relationship. But as I did back then, I ignored the red flags and proceeded to get to know him anyway.

The first six weeks of getting to know each other seemed to progress nicely but then when I spent an evening at his place, with him and his daughter, something caused a big change. He couldn't strip the sheets quick enough in the morning, rushed me out of the house as fast as he could, and hardly contacted me at all during the day. I couldn't work out what I had done wrong. Had I farted in my sleep? Spent too long in the shower? Or was it something else altogether?

I wasn't sure what happened and of course with him pulling away, seeming colder than usual, and not responding to my contact the way he usually would, I began to fear the worst. I started to become extremely scared of what I knew was ahead – abandonment. But what I was really scared of was that empty alone feeling that comes after abandonment – having no-one message you good morning and good night, and no-one to share little stories with or have a cuddle with on the lounge. I was terrified of facing that 'alone' feeling once again, and also anxious about what was going to eventuate – I needed to know what was happening, what was *going* to happen, and when it would happen.

The sensible thing to do in the situation would have been to give Unavailable Teacher some space as he was obviously going through his own stuff (something about having someone share his space and his time with his daughter had triggered something for him), but fear and the need-to-know overwhelmed me and I began to spiral out of control with panic and anxiety. I messaged and phoned him to find out what was going on and he told me that everything was fine, he was just a little busy. But as the week passed and I still hadn't had much contact from him I snapped and ended our relationship during a heated text conversation. It was easier for me to end it now and know where I stood, than to feel the uncertainty and looming darkness. It had got to the point that the anxiety and fear of looming abandonment and emptiness was greater than the pain of abandonment and emptiness itself – ending the relationship prematurely meant I knew what was happening and could feel safe again.

On another occasion it was fear of abandonment which had me at the lowest point I have ever been. I was dating a man, 'Carefree Cop', who openly told me he was hesitant about being in a committed relationship due to his past experiences, and because he was considering relocating for a work promotion when the right opportunity came up. I knew that both these things meant that dating this man came with a high risk of abandonment, but I wasn't at the stage yet where I was strong enough to give up on someone due to the red flags. Because of the situation we were taking things at a slow pace and spending time developing our friendship more than anything else. Little by little I found myself becoming more attached to him and feeling like a future together was a possibility – that was until he phoned me one night to tell me that a job opportunity had become available five hours away. I found it hard to control my fear of losing another person who I had become attached to and became upset on the phone. We ended the phone call on good terms but I started to get the dark feeling of pending abandonment come over me. My anxiety about the situation and my feeling of not knowing what was going to happen plunged me into depression which became worse when I didn't hear from him the next day.

Two days after the phone call I needed to take my children to my older son's AFL game and then we planned to drive 1.5 hours to Melbourne for a family birthday party. I started the day off by trying to be positive and texting Carefree Cop but as the minutes ticked by without a reply I became more and more distressed. Instead of spending time with my children while at the park I spent the morning being devastated and crying inconsolably in a cubicle of the women's toilets. To this day I have the horrifying memory of my younger son banging on the toilet door begging his mummy to let him come in and to 'please stop crying'. For the first time in my life I honestly saw suicide as the only option for ending the repetitive kind of unbearable suffering I experienced in situations like these, and to end the pain my children endured by seeing me in such a state.

Once again my dearest friends rallied around me on the phone to support me, but this time with a higher level of seriousness than ever before, due to me talking about my desire to end my life. The thing saving me from making plans was knowing I had two beautiful children who I loved and who loved me back, and who needed their mum.

Similarly to my experience with Unavailable Teacher I sent Carefree Cop a text message to end the relationship. Knowing it was over was far less painful than the uncertainty of 'not knowing' and the fear of pending abandonment.

Needing to put an end to potential relationships because of the anxiety and distress I felt about the possibility of abandonment led me to prematurely end the opportunity to get to know people who may have been quite lovely and maybe even perfect for me. 'Entitled Plumber' and I shared an amazing date and had planned to see each other again the next week. I really liked him. He was fun, easy-going, extremely attractive and intelligent. Unfortunately, he needed to cancel the next date as he accidentally double booked with a family function, and then he cancelled the following date at late notice because he unexpectedly needed to mind his daughter. In hindsight I can see that they are both reasonable reasons for cancelling a date, but the fear that this was his way of abandoning me left me inconsolable. My close friend, Marcus, couldn't understand why I was so upset about a couple of cancelled dates with a man I had met once. I can see now how irrational it seems, but at the time I was feeling terrified that this person, who I felt such a strong connection with, would disappear from my life. The only way I could manage that situation was to put an end to the uncertainty and anxiety. After hours of crying about the second cancelled date I ended the uncertainty by sending him a 'fuck off' text message.

Now to explain a fuck off text message - a term that my close friends are aware of. A fuck off text message doesn't really say those words, but it is a text making it clear to the other person that I don't want to see them again, and that they have hurt me! The fuck off text message also does a great job of letting the other person know that I am emotionally unstable (or in dating terminology, a 'crazy bitch'). It does the job of keeping them away from me so there is no more uncertainty for me around the role they might play in my life.

I always felt regret after I sent a fuck off text as I realised it was a way of sabotaging any chance I had at developing a relationship with this person. The only purpose was to stop my own fear about what hurt could lie ahead. I realised that I needed to find another way of managing those intense feelings of uncertainty without letting the other person know what I was experiencing.

How do we change our harmful coping strategies? I changed this strategy by realising the damage it was doing. I realised that this coping strategy for the uncertain early stages of a relationship was stopping me from developing relationships by literally scaring men away. I wanted to be able to have a normal relationship bad enough that I needed to look at my unhealthy behaviours.

Over time I found ways of managing the anxiety and fear without letting the other person know about it. My closest friends have spent countless hours on the phone and texting me to help me see situations rationally. Over and over my friends would convince me to see that I needed to be patient, to get on with my day, to think about other things when anxiety sets in, and ultimately that sending a fuck-off message would be unhelpful.

I found that ending the relationship in my head (without telling the other person about it) was also a great way to move through the pain and uncertainty. I would delete their text messages so I didn't have to read them repeatedly, change their name in my phone to something disrespectful like Smug Lawyer, Entitled Plumber, and Grumpy Tradie (yes, there really is a story behind the names I have used for the men in this book), or all together delete their number and any contact I had for them (if I heard from them again – great. If not, it didn't matter because I had made my mind up that the relationship was over from my end).

All this was going on while the other person had no idea that anything was wrong because to let them know of my fear, panic, and anxiety would have been to put me at risk of abandonment. Funnily enough on most occasions I would receive a message or phone call from them less than an hour after I decided to 'silently' delete them from my life (it was a nice surprise and a sign that I had overreacted) and I would continue with the relationship as though nothing had happened (and really it hadn't – apart from in my head).

Over time I have learnt to manage the fear of abandonment in other ways. I learnt to manage my anxiety and eventually to not be so scared of that empty alone feeling, mostly through meditation and self-soothing. As I became happier with my life in general and better at managing my own emotions, the fear of abandonment wasn't such a big deal – I eventually learnt I would be ok even if I did end up on my own. This all helped my behaviours in relationships to become more stable and less impulsive – I was taking another step toward undoing BPD.

Chapter 6

Codependency

I had my first serious boyfriend, Daniel, when I was 18 years old and we were like two peas in a pod. We did everything together, we saw each other every day, we were reliant on each other, and over time the line between who he was and who I was became blurred. I thought it was wonderful to be intertwined with another person like that. But now, when I think about that relationship, I think – codependence.

Codependence in a relationship is when one person relies on the other for meeting their emotional and self-esteem needs. A person who is codependent might feel responsible for their partner's feelings, blame their partner for their own feelings, feel threatened or upset by their partner's opinion or mood, and try to control their partner because they need other people to behave in a certain way to feel ok about themselves.

My friend, Dianne, introduced me to the term codependency while I was dating Grumpy Tradie. She happened to visit me while I was being 'punished' by Grumpy Tradie for something which I innocently said to him.

Grumpy Tradie and I met not long after I separated from my husband. It's safe to say that I was vulnerable and my life was quite messy at the time we met, there were constant arguments with my ex about how and when we each spent time with our children and I was miserable quite a lot of the time while trying to rebuild my future. I thought Grumpy Tradie may have felt an obligation to stick around even though things were chaotic and probably wouldn't progress the way a relationship normally would. After a few weeks of getting to know each other I said to him out of care and concern, "I understand if my situation is too messy and complicated for you to want to be involved any further. Just know, I will be ok if you decide this isn't for you."

Grumpy Tradie's response to what I said was extreme. He became instantly upset, angry and deeply offended. My innocent statement resulted in him arguing with me over three days about how much I had hurt him, and with him saying that if I 'wanted to dump him' I should just get it over with. What happened is that my comment had triggered Grumpy Tradie's insecurities about being in a relationship and instead of owning those feelings he blamed me for them - he was codependent.

In hindsight, I wish I had 'dumped him' then and there; if only I knew how toxic that kind of behaviour was and how abusive it was to become. What happened instead was that I got a lesson from Dianne about codependence. Going on to see full-blown codependence being lived out in my relationship with Grumpy Tradie opened my eyes to the fact that I was also codependent in my relationships (just not to the same degree).

The biggest sign of my codependence in relationships has been expecting my partner to soothe my emotions. If I was upset or anxious about something, for example, an issue at work or with a friend, I thought it was my partner's role to make me feel better about it - whether that was by talking it through with me, giving me a hug, or fixing the problem. Of course, it is great to get support from your partner when you are having a difficult time but it certainly isn't their role to fix the problem and take away all the pain. Like many people I also believed it was normal to take your bad mood out on your partner - as though they were somehow responsible or needed to be made accountable for every negative experience I had.

In return I often found myself with partners who expressed their codependence by getting upset when we did things separately. Instead of seeing separate interests as a sign that we were both healthy, happy, functioning adults they saw it as a sign that the relationship was weakened by our independence from each other.

A one-year relationship with Grumpy Tradie was as good as a Phd in codependence – I learnt all about the dangers, the signs, and the motivations. You would think that by the end of this time I would have eradicated codependency from my make-up, and when it came to the day to day happenings in relationships I did. I was less inclined than ever to get angry at someone because of the way I was feeling about something else, to depend on another person to 'make me happy', or to sit back and accept it when a person gets angry at me or blames me because my opinions or beliefs upset them. But when I looked at my opinions and beliefs around relationships codependence was still there and was stopping me from living my life fully and freely.

How was codependence still there for me? During my dating phase I was lucky to live a flexible life as I worked from home (I could do my work when it suited me – during the day, at night, or on weekends) and I had no solid commitments except of course my children. This flexibility meant I could adjust my schedule to suit any situation. I saw this as a great advantage because it meant I could be flexible in a relationship – if I met someone who worked night shift I could keep my days free to spend with him, if they worked day shift I could work during the day and keep nights free. Even when it became time for me to find more work, I was reluctant to lock in any commitments until I met the right person. What if I found a night shift worker who lived one hour north of me, and I had just committed to a day time role one hour south of where I lived?

It was more than just the work situation. My kids desperately wanted a dog. But what if we had a dog join our family and I met someone who was allergic to dogs or someone who lived far away and having a dog made it difficult to travel to see him on weekends?

One of the challenges with BPD is in developing a stable self-image or sense of who we are. This makes people with BPD vulnerable to codependence because we are less sure about who we are and therefore more willing to change our identity, goals, beliefs, and way of living to fit in with someone else. This is certainly what I was doing when I decided that I would hold off on making any big decisions and I would just live in limbo until I met the right person. When I met 'him' I could then get the 'right' job with the right hours and right location to suit our lifestyle (and only then could I get my financial situation sorted out) and I could then get the 'right' pet to suit all our needs... and as it goes 'we would live happily ever after'.

It wasn't until after one epic failed dating experience that I realised I had enough of waiting for what may never happen. The man I had been dating, 'Egocentric Chef' was consumed with plans for a restaurant he was opening and had very little time to spend with me. I realised that I was repetitively getting to know men who were making big decisions for their lives which excluded me from the bigger picture while I was keen to be a part of their plans for the future and to include them in mine. I realised that other people were getting their lives sorted out while I was waiting for something that may never happen, and it was time to live.

Within one week of this relationship ending I bought a dog for our family and found myself a new job (two days a week and two hours south of where I lived). Suddenly my life became full and more enjoyable than ever. Being busier and having a purpose beyond my household, children, and the job I did from home was rewarding and I felt accomplished and proud of what I was doing.

The funny thing is that while I had been resisting these changes for years because I was afraid they might make 'finding the right man' challenging, instead they actually made dating less difficult and scary.

No longer was I able to instantly adapt to the needs of someone else. I had far less time to spend on dating sites and with less time available I was choosier about who I got to know. When I came across someone who wanted to meet me they needed to wait more than a couple of days before I had time to fit them in. And, if they cancelled the date at the last minute I didn't really mind and instead relished in some time to myself. When it didn't work out with someone I was getting to know, gone was the devastation because now my life was full and happy and rewarding regardless of their potential place in it. As my dear friend Leah told me many times to help me realise that a relationship wasn't 'everything', "Your pie is now almost complete with only one small piece missing."

My change in thinking and getting rid of a codependent way of living was lifesaving. What a change in attitude from the person I was only months before who would drop everything for the opportunity to get to know someone and had everything riding on the possibility that they might be the 'right' person – even whether my kids could get a pet dog.

Chapter 7

Emotional deprivation

Always wanting more. That is the best way I can explain emotional deprivation.

Emotional deprivation is when it doesn't matter how much love, time, and energy someone gives you, you never feel 'loved' and you always need more.

Being in a relationship with someone who has emotional deprivation is exhausting. Having emotional deprivation is exhausting. I have been on both sides of this.

Emotional deprivation is a concept my psychologist introduced me to when we analysed my lifetraps. In the book 'Reinventing Your Life', which explains schemas and lifetraps, emotional deprivation is defined as, "The belief that your need for love will never be met adequately by other people. You feel no one truly cares for you or understands how you feel." Some of the ways emotional deprivation comes across for people is feeling like something is missing, a feeling of emptiness, being demanding or 'needy' in relationships, and feeling like people always let you down.

Emotional deprivation is one of the most common lifetraps in people who have BPD. Our chronic feelings of emptiness and fear that people close to us will leave us, have us constantly needing more love, attention, and reassurance in relationships.

I best relate to emotional deprivation in my marriage. I know that I love to talk and am best suited to a partner who also likes to talk. Constant conversation used to be very important to me in relationships because it helped me to feel connected; at the first sign of silence I would ask questions like, "What is wrong?" "Have I done something wrong?" and "Are you angry at me?"

What I didn't realise is there is a point where silence in a relationship is important and normal too, for example, it is ok to do your own thing around the house for a couple of hours without talking to each other, to watch a show just cuddled up without having to say a word, or for the other person to have thoughts going through their mind which they want to keep to themselves. I didn't manage silence well, it made me feel as though I wasn't loved, something was missing, and I needed more. How exhausting to be with someone who needed to talk all the time because they didn't feel loved enough (and the reality is still wouldn't feel loved enough no matter what you did).

Like all lifetraps, when we have them we do things to ensure they become the reality for our current and future situations. I certainly did this in my marriage. Being so demanding in the relationship pushed my husband away – and guess what? He then started to show less love and less care, and was even less likely to want to talk to me – making emotional deprivation an even greater reality for me.

The combination of feeling so unloved in my relationship with my husband (due to my own issues with emotional deprivation) and with him them distancing himself from me (because I was so demanding) meant I was left with a big void where I felt very unloved and lonely. Being deprived of the connection I needed had me craving a connection. Over time I started to see any small indication of connection from another male as a sign that they would be able to meet my emotional needs, and I started to believe I was falling in love with them. The result of this was that I developed crushes on random men, for example, the man who presented at the conference which I told my friend, Jamie, about (as I described in the prologue). As a result I found myself 'falling in love' again, and again, and again.

When I became single and especially once I realised what codependence was, understanding that I alone am responsible for my happiness helped to reduce the impact of emotional deprivation in my life. When I feel lonely or insecure in a relationship I can look at it logically by asking myself if this is about my issues (me always wanting more), or about the other person genuinely not meeting my needs. However, it isn't always easy to work out the difference especially when you have become wired to feeling deprived. Take the situation with Unavailable Teacher for an example. There I was sailing along in the relationship when I started to feel needy and as though I needed 'more'. Knowing that I have a tendency for needing 'more' because of my emotional deprivation lifetrap I tried to control my own feelings of distress when he went quiet for a week. Was the insecurity I felt because of my own issues or was he genuinely depriving me of my emotional needs in a relationship? I would say that in this case he was depriving me of my emotional needs by disappearing from the relationship without explanation (but expecting the relationship to continue).

The theory is that emotional deprivation comes from not having our emotional needs completely met when we were a young child. In some cases this can be due to severe abuse and neglect, in others it can be subtle things like not being cuddled enough, not feeling listened to, and not being given enough time and attention. On a very basic level I think some of mine came from having a younger sibling quite close in age - how could my parents really fulfil my needs for love, time and affection when there was a younger child in the family who would have needed my parents more than I did for basic everyday things? I also wouldn't be surprised if I was a very demanding child and was wired to be more needy or sensitive than other children, meaning that even if I got the same amount of attention from my parents as other kids did from theirs it may still have fallen short from being what I required (while it would have been ample for other kids).

The irony of emotional deprivation is that when we have this lifetrap we tend to choose partners who are cold and aloof, probably because this type of distance in a relationship feels familiar to what we experienced as a child. I know that while dating, I found I was naturally attracted to men who were emotionally unavailable, and freaked out by men who were present and gave me a lot of time and attention – too many text messages or talking about the future often had me wanting to run away. As I became aware of this pattern I made an effort to devote more time to getting to know men who were in the second group. But time and time again because I wasn't used to being with men who were emotionally available that level of sharing, affection and desire to connect freaked me out, felt over the top and possessive. Was it possessive, or not? Who knows? While I was trying to change my dating ways I found I was constantly confused about what was normal and what wasn't.

In my relationship with my partner emotional deprivation rears its head from time to time and tries to cause havoc.

Sometimes when things are going great, something small (which I know shouldn't bother me) will start to play on my mind, for example, a thought that his ex is more attractive than me, or that I am not valuable to him because I am not a great cook or have more body fat now than I did when I first met him. As a result, I become quiet and introverted. Of course, I can't share with Josh what is bothering me (because I realise it is an irrational, unhealthy and unnecessary thought) but this means he doesn't understand why I am suddenly more quiet than usual – which ends with both of us being quieter than usual and a general feeling of discomfort. As with all life traps the result is that I have created a self -fulfilling prophecy – my weirdness results in him being quieter than usual which creates distance between us and means I don't get my emotional needs met and end up feeling emotionally deprived.

Once I started to see the pattern which was happening I learnt to tell the thoughts about small irrelevant things to 'shut-up'. When a thought which is trying to cause chaos in my relationship enters my mind I think of it like a naughty parrot on my shoulder – I tell the 'parrot' to go away and I ignore what he is saying. This has been a great tactic, but once again emotional deprivation has its way of getting through. Sometimes I now notice that I am quiet and irritated even though there are no specific thoughts going through my head – as though I want to start a fight for no reason. I am still trying to work out whether this is my way of adapting to normal and healthy silence or if emotional deprivation is trying to find another way to ruin my relationship. Until I work this out being aware of the way I feel and trying extra hard to control the way I behave when I feel a little 'off' has been crucial to staying calm, stable, and having a healthy relationship.

Chapter 8

Self-soothing

Self-soothing is s a term you may have heard of relating to babies.

When babies cry and can't fall asleep parents can help to soothe them in many ways. It might help to cuddle them, feed them, give them a dummy, pat or stroke their forehead, take them for a walk or drive, or sing them a song. As a child gets older we may help to soothe them when they are upset by putting their favourite television show on, giving them a cuddle, or giving them something yummy to eat, but in an ideal world we would begin to teach them ways of calming themselves down or soothing themselves – self-soothing.

As an adult it is important we know how to calm ourselves down when we are upset.

People with BPD find it challenging to manage stressful situations and often have very poor self-soothing skills. Instead of calming ourselves down in healthy ways we may become inconsolable, angry, upset and irrational, or turn to unhealthy things to manage the stress like obsessions to certain behaviours, or addictions, for example, to drugs, sex or alcohol.

My self-soothing skills have always been almost non-existent. When I was a child I would have extreme tantrums about the silliest of things, and as a teenager and in my early twenties whenever I felt angry I would cry, scream, and sometimes throw things. I slowly learnt to control my behaviour as I got older because I saw the negative affect it had on others and my relationships with them, I didn't want to be known as an irrational person who threw items across her office (yes, I did once throw a heavy hole-puncher across my office and it only just missed an expensive glass cabinet). However, when it came to extremely stressful situations, especially those related to relationships I still had little control, that was until my wise friend, Dianne, mentioned the term, 'self-soothing'. Just knowing that such a thing existed made me realise that I alone am in control of my emotions and I can't expect anyone else to fix a bad day or bad mood for me.

When I was married I used to drive my husband crazy whenever there was a situation which I felt uneasy about, for example, if I was concerned about something which happened at work. I would constantly talk to him about the situation and expect that he continue to talk to me until I felt completely at ease about it. Whenever we had a big fight (and there were many of them) I would cry inconsolably and then I would get even angrier at him when he wouldn't stay with me to help me calm down. I later realised that it was never his job to make me feel better or to calm me down – that was my job. I needed to learn to self-soothe.

As adults, we have many options for soothing ourselves and calming ourselves down when we are upset.

My need for self-soothing strategies was at its height while I was in my relationship with Grumpy Tradie and regularly subjected to his abusive behaviour. My poor coping mechanisms meant I often tried to control the distress I was feeling and calm myself down by self-harming, another very common behaviour of people with BPD. When I was very distressed I would burn my arms with a cigarette lighter. Watching the flame and feeling and smelling my skin singe somehow helped to calm me down. I also went through a phase when I tried to self-soothe by distracting myself with social media, or texting and phoning my friends (constantly). Although this was a great distraction from the emotions I was feeling it resulted on a heavy reliance on others to calm me down, as well as developing an addiction to my mobile phone and social media.

I learnt that it is important to have a 'kit' of healthy strategies available for self-soothing so that when we are distressed we will have a range of tools we can use.

Some of my strategies for when I feel the anxiety building in my life and things are getting a bit hard for me to manage is to take myself to the beach to meditate quietly, lock myself in the bathroom for a bath, or spend some time reading or writing. These are great pre-emptive steps too. If I get onto them early enough, when I feel that I am becoming anxious about something, I can avoid a full-blown collapse.

One of the more interesting and primitive methods of self-soothing which I have developed is to stroke my own hair, as a parent would to a child. This was something I had always done when I was extremely upset but only later recognised as an attempt to self-soothe.

As I have become better at self-soothing I have become less of a burden on my partners and I feel like a complete and whole individual who can manage her own emotions and behaviour.

The biggest challenge for me has been managing the emotions I feel when I am scared of being abandoned and of being left alone with that horrible heavy empty feeling. I started to feel like I had a handle on most things but wasn't sure how I was ever going to manage that kind of situation until my friend, Clare, suggested that I face it head on! She suggested that being lonely couldn't really hurt me, feeling alone and feeling empty was just a feeling – did I really need to be so terrified of it?

I decided I was ready to tackle the empty feeling and started practising self-soothing in the presence of emptiness – not while I was experiencing extreme stress or trauma, but just every day. I practised lying on my bed alone at night when it was quiet and allowing myself to experience the emptiness. At first I wanted to run from it - to check my phone, stroke my forehead, or cuddle a pillow - but I resisted the urge and forced myself to 'feel' the emptiness.

Lying there in stillness I discovered that emptiness felt like a thick blanket which hovered about ten centimetres above me. The blanket started at my feet and made its way up my body. The blanket of emptiness always hovered above my body but first it covered my feet, then legs, then torso and continued until it reached my neck. And, when it reached my neck it settled down on me like a heavy quilt. At first the feeling was terrifying but as I laid there and breathed through the anxiety I realised that the emptiness wasn't a danger. It was heavy, it consumed me and made it hard for me to move with its heavy weight upon my body - but it couldn't hurt me. Over time I learnt to breathe and relax with the feeling of emptiness upon me. And with practise I became quicker at relaxing in the presence of the emptiness. Eventually I found there was something empowering about being there alone with just my blanket of emptiness and loneliness, and feeling complete. This technique soon became another tool in my kit of strategies for self-soothing.

One of the first times I realised the power of this method was when I had some news which was devastating to me - that a man I had been involved with, Entitled Plumber, wasn't interested in developing a relationship with me (Yes, you may remember Entitled Plumber from the chapter on fear of abandonment. Well he and I reunited several times long after the first episode of when I was 'abandoned' after a single date).

Entitled Plumber and I had been spending quite a bit of time together over a period of about three months. I realised we weren't an official couple but we seemed to be getting closer to each other and were seeing each other about twice a week. I was devastated one night when I told him that I had missed him over the weekend and his response was, "You shouldn't be missing me, you should be out partying." I asked, "And if I did go out partying and met someone, how would you feel?" He told me, "I'd be glad to see you happy." The conversation went on and it became clear that Entitled Plumber wasn't interested in me for anything more than someone to have casual sex with, whereas I had always had feelings for him and thought we were developing into something more.

I was devastated. I still stayed at his house that night and slept next to him but I put my blanket of emptiness over me. The old me would have cried all night, showed him how angry I was at him and demanded he talk to me about the situation. This new me – with emotional control, and self-soothing techniques – laid down next to him, put my blanket of emptiness over me, and slept despite being heart-broken and upset.

As traumatic a night as that was for me, because I was devastated that I had been rejected by a man who I was in love with, I also felt triumphant. The fact that I could self-soothe meant I had handled a traumatic situation with dignity rather than becoming an emotional mess, and was able to walk away with my pride intact. I felt I had mastered the art of self-soothing.

My tips for self-soothing

Things which help to soothe me include:

- Having a bath
- Meditating
- Patting my own hair
- Patting my dog
- Watching a movie
- Reading a book
- Having a nap
- Wearing comfortable clothes and getting cosy on the lounge with a cup of tea
- Going for a walk on the beach
- Pulling out grass

Chapter 9

Addiction

Addiction isn't a nice word. When you hear the word addiction what do you think of? Many people think of the big things, the things that cause havoc in society, perpetuate violence and rip families apart...

drug addiction,

alcohol addiction,

sex addiction,

gambling addiction.

You might also think of addictions that cause damage to individuals making it hard for them to stay healthy and happy...

smoking addiction,

exercise addiction,

shopping addiction,

coffee addiction.

Addiction is a condition that results when a person uses a substance or engages in an activity that can be pleasurable but becomes compulsive and interferes with ordinary responsibilities and concerns, such as work, relationships, or health. Addictions come in all shapes and sizes. Some have bigger implications than others, but at the heart of an addiction is a coping mechanism, something people do to escape reality.

The relationship between addiction and BPD has been described as a volatile one. Addictions are common in people who have BPD because they provide a way of distracting and numbing the pain from difficult emotions. Unfortunately, the addiction can then worsen the difficulties related to BPD. For example, excessive use of alcohol or drugs can make it harder for the person to be in control of their emotions and cause an increase in erratic behaviours; and addictions to sex or spending can result in considerable guilt, and lack of self-worth. Ultimately, many addictions have the effect of creating more pain and difficult emotions; creating a vicious cycle of continuing with the addictive behaviour to numb the pain.

I consider myself extremely fortunate to have not had any addictions impact me in a significant way. My innocent dependence on coffee when I was in my early 30's was my first taste of the power of addiction and even then, at its worst, I only had one coffee a day. Initially I would have a coffee with a sweet treat in the afternoon two or three times a week, then it became most afternoons, and soon I noticed that when it came to about 3.30pm I would get jittery, irritated and found it impossible to concentrate – all I could think about was my coffee and cake!

Most people would say that one coffee a day is no big deal (and compared to the seriousness of many other addictions such as alcohol and drug addictions, I absolutely see that point of view) but I hated that I was reliant on something to get me through the day. Once I realised that I was dependant on my coffee and sugar hit I stopped cold turkey! That afternoon instead of buying my usual afternoon snack I purchased a fresh vegetable juice and some nuts, and slowly the afternoon cravings ceased. I still get a little edgy around 3.30 in the afternoons, but I have replaced the 'unhealthy' dependence with something which is healthier for me.

I wish I could say my next addiction was as easy to manage! Again, I understand that my addictions are insignificant compared to what many others experience but I think my story shows how an innocent coping mechanism (and an attempt to self-soothe) can become problematic.

During the later years of my marriage and especially in the first few years of being single I developed a phone addiction! At any moment of being upset or distressed I would turn to my phone for distraction. Child misbehaving... boyfriend say something a little bit strange... weighed myself and I was heavier than usual... checked my bank balance and there was less money there than I thought there would have been... had a mental block when it came to my wedding invitation work – and I was straight to my phone to instantly take my mind off the distressing thoughts. With Facebook, text messages, dating apps (when I was single), email, and friends to phone, my mobile phone allowed an instant distraction to take my mind off the things I didn't want to face. Sometimes I would pick my phone up more than 20 times in an hour looking for a distraction and something to soothe my anxiety.

My phone addiction was problematic because checking my phone so many times in a day meant there was little time for anything else. It got in the way of completing my work, managing my home, having meaningful interactions and conversations with my kids, and with developing strategies to manage issues in a productive way (like learning how to manage my anxiety rather than avoiding it by using my phone).

When I realised I had a phone dependence I decided to face it head on in the same way I faced my coffee dependence, with instant 'detox'. The problem was that I couldn't just get rid of my phone because I needed it for my everyday activities. Instead I needed to cut down on my use.

It doesn't matter where you go these days, you will see people using their phones. People are on their phones in the waiting room at the doctors, while waiting for a bus or train, and at school pickups while waiting for their kids to finish school. While some of them may be using the time to be productive, for example to pay bills, communicate with a friend, or play a game they enjoy, many people use their phone as a time filler.

My detox from my phone was about making sure that I only used it when there was a purpose - not just for the sake of it. Instead of checking my phone throughout the day I decided to have some guidelines around when I could use it. I decided I would spend 10 minutes on my phone when I woke in the morning, 30 minutes after lunch, and 30 minutes in the evening. Of course, if I got an important text message I could reply, but there was to be no more just starting a text conversation with someone because I needed a 'phone connection hit', no more checking Facebook to see how many notifications there were since the last time I checked (25 minutes ago), and no more replying to every message I received on a dating app minutes after they came through.

My first day of overcoming my phone addiction was hard. I remember literally shaking, finding it hard to breathe and tapping my fingers incessantly at the times when I would usually 'phone a friend'. Instead I needed to sit with whatever was worrying me and 'feel' it, for example, if I was anxious because my boyfriend said something a bit confusing I needed to let myself feel the anxiety instead of covering it up with the distraction of my phone. Sitting with the anxiety always felt impossible at first, but after five minutes or so the anxiety decreased and became more tolerable.

The key to overcoming an addiction for me was understanding what my dependence was and what made me turn to it. I then needed to see what negative effect it was having on my life. Understanding these impacts was a great motivation for overcoming my addiction. And the more I overcame it the more resilient I became, and better I became at being able to manage my anxiety in more healthy ways.

Chapter 10

Unrelenting standards

Middle ground isn't a place I am familiar with. I have always been much more comfortable with a 'black and white', 'all or nothing', and 'succeed or fail' way of thinking.

Because of this way of thinking I have always strived for perfection and considered anything less than perfection as a failure. I can see now that this way of thinking has made life tougher for me than it needed it to be.

In my work with my psychologist we found that another lifetrap I had was the 'unrelenting standards' life trap. People with unrelenting standards strive to meet extremely high expectations of themselves; place excessive emphasis on status, money, achievement, beauty, order or recognition; and often apply their high standards of themselves to other people as well, so can be very judgemental. I could see how this lifetrap related to me especially when it came to having high expectations of myself, and placing excessive emphasis on achievement, beauty (related to body image problems), and order. I could also see how this theme consumed so many areas of my life and from such a young age with the early signs being I was impatient and a perfectionist.

When I was in my early teens I remember my parents mentioning that we would buy new furniture for my bedroom, so I demanded we go furniture shopping that weekend. When

I was a little older, in my late teens, I was the driving force for my mum to buy a house. Again, I remember that she mentioned she was thinking about buying a house rather than renting, and I said, "Well, let's go and look for one." We looked at houses with real estate agents for the next three days and before my mum even had time to work out her home loan properly she was putting in an offer for a house. Growing up I always prided myself on being a driving force for getting my parents to act on things – I didn't at the time realise it was a sign of impatience.

Impatience is a trait I have always had although I didn't understand why. I can now see that I am impatient because I expect nothing but the best of myself and others and when I make a decision I like to move toward putting the plan into action as soon as possible. This is a part of my unrelenting standards lifetrap.

When it came to my university years perfectionism was apparent. I wasn't one of those students who could do just enough to pass. I gave every assignment, exam or assessment task 100% because I didn't understand how to do any different. It meant that I got great grades and the lecturers loved me but it also meant that I spent way more time doing university work than I needed to in order to obtain my degree – sacrificing the time I could have been spending doing more enjoyable things such as time with my friends and family.

Parenting was another area where perfectionism reared its head. My idea of the early years of parenting was to spend lots of time with my kids doing things like craft, cooking and reading; and to spend my 'me' time exercising and keeping fit. But after my first son was born and I started to develop close friendships with other mums I started to become influenced by their strengths as parents. One mum managed to be a great mum while finding time to go out for lunch with her girlfriends, another made amazing hand-made gifts for all the children's birthdays, another looked amazing every day in designer clothing, then there was one who made different and interesting meals for her family every night, and Laura (who I have already mentioned) was a housework extraordinaire who managed to find time to relax with a glass of wine at the end of the day.

My tendency to have an unstable image of who I was (related to the BPD) as well as my drive to meet very high expectations of myself (because of the unrelenting standards lifetrap) meant that I believed I wasn't good enough. For a long time I believed that to be a 'good enough' parent and wife I needed to do craft, reading and cooking with my kids, make time to have lunch with my girlfriends, make hand-made gifts and craft items, wear designer clothing, cook gourmet meals, and have a spotless house all while having time to sit on the lounge at the end of the day to relax. I felt I needed to take the strengths of each of my friends and become just as accomplished in every single area. Worse still, not only did I want to take on all of their strengths but I believed that anything less wasn't good enough, and I caused myself a lot of stress and anxiety trying to reach such high expectations of myself as a parent, wife, and home keeper.

When it came to relationships my expectations for what is and isn't acceptable have always been very high. One fight, argument, or difference of opinion and my immediate response has always been, 'What's the point? We might as well end it now." One of the men I dated (of course it was Smug Lawyer) pointed out that I had quite high standards for myself but I shouldn't expect others to live up to them too.

In my work with my psychologist my high standards became apparent as we would discuss a new coping strategy or I would learn a new perspective on things. After learning a new strategy I would get angry at myself when I struggled to make the changes instantly, or if the improvements took a while to occur.

As I learnt about my unrelenting standards and the impact they were having on my life I tried to be gentler with myself. I realised that everybody makes mistakes, that things took time to happen, and that it was important to celebrate achievements along the way to reaching your final goal or destination. I slowly came to give up on the black and white way of thinking and adopted a more 'grey' approach – I was finally learning to do middle ground. And middle ground is a wonderful place to be for a person with BPD.

With the extremes of emotions and struggles with relationships that people with BPD experience, learning to do middle ground is essential to stability and survival. Middle ground means that we can be devastated about a relationship break up but still be happy and content because other aspects of our life are going well. It means that when a relationship fails we can see it for what it is (a relationship that didn't work out) rather than seeing it as indication that we are failures as human beings. It means that even if our partner doesn't meet 100% of our needs we can still enjoy being with them and building a future with them because we realise that there is no such thing as a perfect relationship.

Doing 'grey' and getting rid of the all or nothing, black and white, and succeed or fail mentality, was a gift. Life has become far less stressful for me since trying to look at things this way as I can see that even when things aren't going as well (or progressing as quickly) as I had hoped there is always something else to be happy about.

My tips for managing unrelenting standards

- I remind myself that everything takes time and focus on 'practising being patient' - 'Rome wasn't built in a day'.
- I decide what is a realistic goal, achievement or investment and set my sights on working toward that. I am conscious about celebrating my achievements without rushing to choose a higher milestone to work toward.
- I remind myself that it is ok to be sad about something but still happy about other aspects of my life.
- I challenge my 'black and white' and 'all or nothing' views by asking what will really happen if I land somewhere in the middle.
- I try to be gentle on myself and forgive myself when I don't achieve what I am hoping to.
- I try to be gentle on others by seeing the positive things they are doing and their positive intentions, rather than focussing on areas for improvement.

Chapter 11

Mindfulness

"Mindfulness is the basic human ability to be fully present, aware of where we are and what we are doing, and not overly reactive or overwhelmed by what is going on around us."

Mindfulness meditation is one of the only methods I have found which helps to manage my anxiety. I was sceptical when mindfulness was first suggested to me as something I could do to help reduce the intensity of my anxiety, as well as something I could do to decrease how often I felt anxious. Being a big believer in science and medicine, mindfulness seemed like some kind of wishy-washy alternative therapy and I couldn't understand how it could possibly 'fix' a brain problem like anxiety. But the more I read about mindfulness meditation the more I found that the science and evidence was there.

Mindfulness isn't just any kind of meditation. It is a practice of becoming aware of the present and accepting it without judgement. When meditating in this way you sit quietly with your eyes open or closed and are aware of your thoughts, your body, and your surroundings without reacting or responding to them. It can be hard to keep your mind still, especially when feeling upset or distressed about something as it is natural to want to think about solutions, go over what has happened, rehash conversations, or think about something totally different to distract from the present. The trick with mindfulness meditation is that when you realise your mind has wandered to gently push the thoughts aside and refocus on the present – what you can hear, see, smell, and feel.

Mindfulness meditation has been shown to reduce stress, anxiety, and depression; help with addiction recovery; and improve concentration and attention. Regular mindfulness meditation has been linked to changes in the brain structure including less aging within the brain tissue; increased thickness in areas of the brain responsible for memory, learning, and emotional regulation; and decreased size in the amygdala, an area of the brain responsible for fear, anxiety and stress. The change which I find most relevant to my experience is that regular mindfulness meditation causes quietening and less activity in areas of the brain responsible for mind wandering. Of course, this makes sense because while meditating we purposefully stop our minds from wandering – it is great to know that the benefits carry over to even while we are not meditating.

From the research, it is clear that the benefits of regular meditation for people with BPD is that it trains our brains to stay calm, to let go of thoughts, and lowers overall anxiety and depression levels. This means that when something goes wrong we are better able to manage the stressful situation. I like to think of regular mindfulness meditation like the maintenance required to look after a car. By regularly cleaning my car, filling it with fuel, and getting it serviced regularly, I know the car will be ready for action when I need to use it. This is opposed to meditating only when I'm highly anxious or pulling the car out in an emergency to find the petrol light is flashing red (in reality I'm not actually very good at maintaining my car and have been caught multiple times with no petrol, but I thought the analogy was a good one).

Now that we have talked about what mindfulness meditation is and the benefits, how do we go about actually doing it?

When I meditate, I like to go to the same spot on the beach near my house, and sit cross-legged while watching the ocean. However, there are times when I have meditated in the big soft chair in my loungeroom with my eyes closed, on the train on the way to the city to meet friends, or in the car when I reach my destination 10 minutes early. Once I have found my spot I switch my phone onto aeroplane mode so I am not interrupted, and set my alarm for five minutes.

Five minutes doesn't seem like a long time when you are playing on your phone, watching TV, or lying in bed pressing snooze, but there are times when it feels longer than long and time spent meditating can be one of them. Renowned author, Elizabeth Gilbert, talks about her struggles with meditation in her book 'Eat Pray Love'. When Elizabeth started meditating she found it a struggle to keep her mind 'still'. Likewise, my mind wanders constantly while meditating. In five minutes of meditation I used to find myself repetitively pushing my thoughts aside to refocus my attention on the present. On some occasions five minutes has seemed so long that I have started to think that the volume on my phone must be too soft or that I forgot to set my alarm – I would interrupt my meditation to check my phone and find there was still around one minute to go!

Over time it became easier to meditate for five minutes with my mind not wandering as much as it used to. Eventually, inspired by a moment in 'Eat Pray Love' where Elizabeth Gilbert had success with meditation and ended up meditating all night long, I decided that I would increase my meditation time – to a less impressive but still beneficial 15 minutes.

At some of the most stressful times of my life (usually when I was feeling very anxious because I was having problems with someone I was dating), I would meditate once or twice a day for up to 15 minutes each time. After meditating I momentarily felt like my troubles were no longer a part of me. It felt as though I had an aura or shield around me and my problems were on the outside and I could just watch them from a distance. Mindfulness meditation was a great strategy to calm myself down and to feel more grounded.

As life has become less stressful for me I have stopped meditating regularly and it has become like a tool in my box of coping strategies – something that I know is reliable and I can use when the stress gets a little too much. However, there are times when I feel compelled to be mindful and do some meditation. On the weekends and while on holidays Josh and I like to spend time together exploring beaches and bush walking tracks. Finding a new lookout with a view of the ocean is something we both love to do. Occasionally, I will find a spot that calls for me to sit and be mindful while taking in the amazing view of the ocean. My partner has become used to me sitting down cross-legged and taking five minutes to myself to just be.

My tips for mindfulness meditation

I do the following to help me get the most benefit from my meditation time.

- Choose a spot where there will be few interruptions (the beach is my favourite spot).
- Turn off distractions, such as the television, and put my phone on silent.
- Decide how long I would like to meditate and set a timer (I always double check that my timer is set correctly so I don't have to interrupt my meditation to check it is working when time seems to go very slow).
- Sit comfortably and gently rest my eyes on something in the distance, or close my eyes.
- Slow down my thoughts by concentrating on my breathing. I am aware of what I am feeling, seeing, hearing, and smelling.
- When I find my mind has wandered and I am thinking about something, I make a decision to stop thinking, and I refocus on my breathing and on what I can feel, see, hear and smell.

Chapter 12

Shame

I was 10 years old and all the other kids were sneaking over to the buffet and helping themselves to a piece of rockmelon from the servery. It had been a long time since I had eaten food from a buffet and my cousins and other kids who were there for dinner that night told me it was fine to go and get a piece of fruit.

We were on a family holiday at a beachside town in southern Victoria, Australia. While on holidays we spent our days at the beach and many of our nights at the local pub. The families we holidayed with often bought dinner at the pub but our family usually had dinner at the tent before heading out to meet up with everyone else.

That evening I edged my head through the row of adults standing at the buffet and stuck my hand out to get a piece of rockmelon, when the lady who worked there scowled at me. She said something about me being a greedy child and stealing food. I felt ashamed to think that she really felt that way about me.

The shame of that incident lived with me for a long time. I couldn't tell any of my cousins or friends back at the table what had happened. Instead I told them I already ate my fruit before I got back to them, no I didn't want to go and get another piece, and no I didn't think my brother should go and get some - it tasted like it was rotten, and I would probably wake up sick from it.

It is an incident that I haven't shared with anyone - until now - and the memory of feeling ashamed, embarrassed and belittled remains fresh in my mind.

Shame is a horrible thing. Shame exists from the silence... from keeping things to ourselves. Author and research professor, Brene Brown, who studies courage, vulnerability, shame and empathy, discusses that talking about our experiences sends shame out of hiding. Talking about things creates connections, and shame hates connections - shame wants us to suffer in silence.

Since my marriage ending most of my shame has been about my failed relationships. When deciding to leave my husband I had to let go of a large amount of guilt and shame about the failed marriage to allow myself to make the final decision to move on.

With dating, I have felt shame and embarrassment at each relationship ending. I can understand that not every man is going to be the right one for me, but after having a few failed relationships and more than a few failed dating experiences I started to ask myself, "What is wrong with me?" and "Why can't I make a relationship work or last?" I started to feel like I was a real loser and wondered if other people felt that way about me too.

The more work I did on myself the more I came to see that 'failed relationships' weren't always because I did something wrong or cause to feel ashamed. One man I was dating, 'Sneaky Smoker' seemed to have all the right qualities to make a good partner but there was something about him I couldn't quite work out - it was as though he was hiding things from me. He seemed to be hiding his views and opinions about things and eventually I found out that he was also hiding that he was a heavy smoker. Smoking is a deal breaker for me when it comes to choosing a partner. Another deal breaker for me is lying.

I strongly believe that when you lie to someone you deny them the opportunity to make their own decisions about their life. My husband lied to me frequently - he lied to me so I wouldn't get angry about things he had done or spent his money on, or mistakes he had made. His lies made me angry for many reasons, the main one being that lying to someone because you are afraid of their response denies them the opportunity to show empathy, forgiveness, and to be loving. By lying my ex-husband showed that he was assuming I would be angry at him rather than allowing me the opportunity to show how caring and understanding I could be.

So, with my aversion to both smoking and lying, when I found out that Sneaky Smoker had been lying to me about smoking I knew I needed to stop dating him. I was angry that I had invested into getting to know this man and started sharing aspects of my life with him, and I felt ashamed that another relationship had failed. I also felt embarrassed that my kids would see me as a failure who couldn't maintain a relationship - who broke up with someone again!

Turning the shame around was hard but eventually I began to see that there was no need for shame in this case - the relationship didn't fail because of something I did (or didn't do) - it failed because of his dishonesty.

My experience with Sneaky Smoker helped me develop faith in my own ability to be a great partner and to do my best in my relationships (even though my best isn't always wonderful).

I have had one other break up since the relationship with Sneaky Smoker and again shame reared its head but in a different way than usual - instead of me shaming myself, this man tried to shame me.

I was dating, 'Angry Courier'. The signs were there that shame was how he played the relationship game. Some people try to make others feel bad about their behaviour by 'shaming them'. Parents do it all the time. Have you ever said to your child, "I expected better from you"? This can have the effect of making a child feel ashamed of their behaviour – maybe that's a good thing – I don't know. But in a relationship shaming the other person, simply because of the way their actions have made you feel is extremely damaging for the relationship.

Angry Courier was a shaming expert, a bit of Facebook stalking prior to getting involved with him revealed some red-flags. There were numerous public posts on his pages which went into great detail about the dramas he was having with his ex-wife and all the things she had done 'wrong' since their break up. I can clearly see how these were signs that Angry Courier uses shaming to make people feel bad when things don't go his way, and I really should have seen this as a sign to stay away from him – but once again I ignored the red flags.

My relationship with Angry Courier ended when he accused me of cheating when I was having a text conversation with a male friend. I hadn't cheated and I had no intention of cheating. Angry Courier told me that what I did to him was incomprehensible and he was sorry he got involved with me. On this occasion, I resisted the temptation to slip back into feeling ashamed. Having a word (shame) to put to what he was trying to do to me, and knowing about his past meant I was strong enough to believe in myself rather than plunge into feeling ashamed.

I see shaming behaviours in relationships all the time. It's about making one person feel bad about their decisions and behaviours, for example one person plans to go out and their partner makes a subtle comment that, "We haven't got enough money to go out for dinner but you found enough to go out with your friends." One of my friends had an experience early on in her relationship when she had a day off work and chose to catch up with a friend. Her new partner made a comment that evening that the floor of her house was dirty and maybe she could have mopped it rather than catching up with her friend. For some reason, he didn't like that she had spent time with her friend and tackled this by trying to make her feel shame about the way she kept her house.

My latest and most significant feeling of shame came from an event that happened when Josh and I first moved in together. I prided myself on having developed so many skills for controlling my own emotions and behaving well in a relationship. Then I had a slip back and was devastated with myself...

Josh and I had just moved in together, into my house, and while everything should have been happy and rosy I was feeling overwhelmed with insecurity. In the lead up to the move I had methodically gone through the house and removed as many remnants of my past relationships as I could so that we could have a fresh start and build our family home together. I made sure that old lingerie got thrown out, gifts from exes got donated to the op shop, and old family photo albums got put away into the back of the cupboard.

As my partner moved his belongings into our new home I found myself obsessing about the story which each of his items held. I wondered if the framed photo of him with his children was taken by an ex on a nice family day out, if the kitchen items were used for them to cook romantic dinners with, and what special event his jewellery was a gift for. But there was one item that I found myself particularly obsessing about. It was one of Josh's expensive remote-control cars and was one of the first things he moved into the house (and straight into our bedroom – "so it didn't get damaged"). I knew that the car was a gift from his ex and having it in constant view when I woke up, got dressed, went to bed, and made love to my partner was exceptionally hard to manage. The obsessive thoughts were consuming me and the more I tried to push them away and ignore them the more they popped into my head. I wasn't comfortable sharing these thoughts with my partner because I knew they were irrational and didn't want him to feel guilty or upset. As a result, I became quiet and withdrawn as I tried to manage these thoughts on my own.

On the first night that Josh officially moved into the house the pressure of managing these kinds of thoughts became too much for me. He was sorting through his things and accidentally left a photo of his ex-wife, on their wedding day, on the top of a pile of photos on my lounge – it was a massive sting I wasn't expecting and all the thoughts I had been trying to hide erupted to the surface in one instant. I felt like I projectile vomited my thoughts out as I screamed and yelled hysterically, letting my partner know how angry I was about the inconsiderate act of leaving the photo out and how angry I was that his beloved remote-control car had prime place in our bedroom. While my partner knew that something had been wrong he was understandably shocked by my extreme reaction as he had no idea these things had been bothering me.

After my outburst of yelling like an uncontrollable fiery dragon I was overwhelmed with shame. I was so embarrassed and ashamed to have let my emotions get the better of me and that I didn't live up to my normal high standards of behaviour. I took myself to bed and cried, and then cried some more. I wanted to stay there and not have to face or speak to Josh ever again.

The feeling of shame is something most people with BPD can relate to. Whether it is shame we feel because of trauma or abuse we endured as a child and would rather not speak about, or shame because we feel guilty and embarrassed about the way we treat others when we become triggered or irrational, shame has devastating effects and is related to the high rates of self-harming and suicide in people with BPD. There have been times when living with the ongoing shame has seemed too hard.

Shame has a wonderful way of keeping us trapped in a bad situation or cycle of problems.

Shame stops us from talking about our problems with others.

Shame stops us from wanting to think about our problems because thinking about them makes us feel uncomfortable and bad about ourselves (and yet, as hard as we try to push the thoughts out of our mind, they pop up and bring horrible feelings with them - just like the rockmelon incident which I hid from for 20 years).

Shame keeps us small and stops us from moving forward and from making better, wiser, and braver decisions.

Shame makes us vulnerable.

When someone else is shaming us, they are doing so to try and keep us smaller than them, to burst our bubble, or to put us in our place.

Brene Brown talks about the antidote for shame being communication. Talking about what makes us feel bad brings it out in the open. When we share what we are going through and other people can relate, it is a great opportunity to help them with their shame, just as it helps us to heal from ours. I have found there is one other antidote to shame... and that antidote is grace.

Chapter 13

Grace

'Grace' is such a significant part of the way I try to live my life that I have the word tattooed on my ribs.

I first heard the word Grace when I was in my 20's and read the book, 'What's so Amazing about Grace?' by Phillip Yancey.

While the book gives a detailed account of the biblical origins of the word, Grace, I took from the book that it is important to be able to forgive others when we feel let down, hurt, or disappointed by their actions (to show them grace), and more significantly, I realised many years later, that we need to be able to forgive ourselves when we are disappointed about the way we behave.

What would you have said to the 10-year-old me who felt bad about herself because she had been scolded for eating a piece of fruit from a buffet? Would you have told her she should feel bad about herself for the next 20 years because what she did was awful? I would like to think that if I was the adult in this situation I would have told the child version of me to forgive herself... she didn't know that what she was doing was 'wrong'. Showing the child care, love, understanding and forgiveness is practising grace.

As someone with unrelenting standards it is very easy for me to beat myself up when I get things 'wrong' – when I yell at my kids, when I make a mistake at work, when I don't get as much done in the day as I would have liked to, when I miss an exercise session, or when I lose my cool in my relationships and am embarrassed by my behaviour.

If I was to let shame have its way I would live in those moments of perceived failure for far too long. Instead of letting shame dominate the way I feel when I 'fail', I remind myself that I am still learning. I often tell myself that because I have never been in the exact situation before (for example, my kids have never been that exact age and pushed my buttons in quite that way before) I can't expect to get things right every time. When it comes to relationships I remind myself that I have never tried so hard and done so well at controlling my emotions before. I acknowledge that there are limits to how much I can manage before my anxiety or insecurities get in the way and that I am bound to get things wrong from time to time, and that's ok! Of course, I still feel upset and ashamed when I behave in ways I am not proud of, but I refuse to beat myself up about it. Instead, I forgive myself and show myself grace, just as I would a small child. This allows me to think about the incident rationally, to learn from it, and move on.

Lots of people feel shame related to their past or present relationships. By the time many people are my age (in their mid 30's) they are picking up the pieces from one or two failed significant relationships. One day while I was listening to random songs on the radio it occurred to me that there are hundreds of songs in existence about relationships. For as long as modern song writing has been a 'thing' people have been writing about love, being in love, finding love, and losing love. Why is this the topic of so many songs? Because relationship problems are common and people have been having the same kinds of issues and concerns for decades. And yet so many people still feel ashamed of the experiences they have had around 'failed' relationships and feel they can't speak freely about them. I have learnt that it is ok to feel scared of relationships, to feel like we don't know what we are doing, and to mess up and to get it wrong. In fact, it is more than ok - it is normal! By talking about our relationship problems, we send out a clear message that YES relationships ARE hard, they aren't perfect and that's ok.

Grace is how I choose to treat myself when I make bad decisions or behave poorly. In forgiving myself for my relationship problems I removed my personal shame and this allowed me to grow as an individual and overcome many of the challenging behaviours I had relating to BPD. By forgiving myself I was also free to share my experiences with others which helps them to see they are not alone in having personal struggles and hopefully encourages them to offer themselves grace.

Sharing our hardships and experiences is necessary for building a community of people who can accept their situation, forgive themselves, and make positive changes. I believe that learning about the concepts in this book has been essential for my healing from BPD, but that ultimately, Grace, is the answer.

Epilogue

Sarah Woods is Unborderline

I am at a gorgeous local beach on a sunny Sunday morning to do a fitness event with my partner. Life is good. I am happily engaged, I have a great job, and I know I am doing my best to be a loving and supportive parent to my two kids and Josh's two children. I feel like I have this juggling act of partnering, working, and parenting, somewhat under control.

Before we start our event, I head over to the toilets at a park near-by. As I walk into the toilets I get a sudden and graphic memory of the last time I was in this same place. It was the memory of two years earlier when I was at one of the lowest points in my life crying in the toilet cubicle and wishing I could put an end to my life.

The memory startled me. Was that really me? Did a dating drama really cause me to want to end my life? Was being in such a state really a regular part of my existence?

Sometimes it is hard to believe how lonely, lost, and vulnerable I used to be. While the memories of some very sad and difficult times in my life are graphic and take me back to those exact moments, it's impossible for me to connect the person I am now to the person I was then. The truth is, it's because I'm not the same person. There is no way that I would now respond to events in the same way I did before my transformation. With the work I have done on myself – the therapy, the reading, reflecting, and forever challenging my thoughts, feelings, and behaviours, I really did build a new me. I unborderlined myself.

What is it like to be unborderline?

Calm

Pride

Gratefulness

Unborderline is about living life with a level of calm, of being in control of my emotions, and feeling proud that I can independently meet my emotional needs. It provides a wonderful feeling of knowing I will be ok no matter what life throws at me.

It is about being aware of where I have come from and being grateful for the opportunities I have had, to recreate my life. While some aspects of my childhood contributed to my challenges, being raised to be independent, resilient and to aim for perfection gave me the strength, courage and determination to demand a better life for myself and the perseverance to do the work to achieve it. Being raised to value friendships and to be a loving and supportive friend meant that I have developed wonderful relationships with people who have in turn supported me to get through the hard times and to make my changes. I am forever grateful for the countless numbers of hours my closest friends spent with me on the phone listening to me cry and talking about the same things every day; for responding to my text messages at all hours of the day and night; and for taking time out of their lives to be there for me at my times of crisis.

Being unborderline is about being grateful for my parent's constant support when I was going through my most challenging years after my separation. While I may not have been comfortable discussing my situation with them in detail, they were always available to provide practical support when needed. From making the 1.5 hour drive to mind my children so I could have a night out, to giving me money so I could afford groceries, pay for a child's excursion, meet my mortgage repayments, or take my children on a holiday, they have always been prepared to help.

Being unborderline also has challenges.

Fear

Responsibility

Exhaustion

Being unborderline is about knowing how challenging life can become, being aware of my fragility and vulnerability, and feeling afraid that I might slip back into darkness when I am confronted with a difficult time in my life.

Being unborderline is about having learnt to see life objectively and trying very hard to not become emotional about things I can't control. This means that I sometimes get accused of being 'uncaring' and 'cold' when I fail to show that I am upset about things which other people may respond to by crying, losing sleep, or being unable to carry on with daily activities.

Being unborderline means that the work is never over. It is a conscious effort to behave appropriately. It means I am constantly aware of what I am thinking, feeling, and how I am acting. This can be tiring.

Being unborderline comes with a great sense of responsibility for the emotional well-being of my children. I am aware that the way I interact with my children can have a profound impact on the way they view themselves in the future, how they manage stressors in their lives, and the way they develop and maintain intimate relationships.

Being unborderline comes with fear that people will use my past against me and fail to see me for who I am now. That they will fail to allow me to make errors or have bad days without attributing it to having had BPD.

Despite the challenges, having experienced BPD for the majority of my adult life and knowing that I have overcome it provides me with a feeling of strength. I wish I could say that making the changes to become unborderline was easy but the truth is we can't create a new way of thinking, feeling, and being without wanting to change, doing the work, and then letting go of the old ways – and letting go of things is never easy.

A note from Sarah Woods

Dear Reader,

Life has it's challenges for all of us. With BPD there are extra challenges which can have their impact in every day situations.

If you are affected by BPD I hope my story has provided some of the knowledge required to make positive changes in your life. I hope it has sparked new ways of thinking and given hope that BPD isn't a life sentence.

If you have a friend or family member with BPD I hope my story has provided some insight into what it is like to live life with this disorder so you can better support them in their darkest moments and on their road to recovery.

Most importantly, I hope this book has helped you to understand that recovery is possible. Know that making small positive changes starts to chip away at unhealthy ways of thinking and acting. Know that little-by-little it's possible to heal from BPD and to become unborderline.

Sarah Woods xx

References

Preface

1. BPD diagnosis

Diagnostic and Statistical Manual of Mental Disorders (DSM-IV)

2. "However, the good news is that even though many people with BPD struggle for a long time, with the right treatment, many recover (some studies have shown that 80% of people stop meeting the criteria for BPD for periods as long as four years, and 50% of people recover completely)"

Alexander L. Chapman. (2011). *Borderline Personality Disorder: Fact and Fiction*. "BPD" issue of Visions Journal. 7 (1).

3. Dialectical Behaviour Therapy

Alexander L. Chapman. (2011). *Borderline Personality Disorder: Fact and Fiction*. "BPD" issue of Visions Journal. 7 (1).

4. Schemas and lifetraps

Jeffrey E. Young and Janet S. Klosko. (1994). *Reinventing Your Life*. Penguin Group: USA.

Chapter 1: Anxiety

5. Anxiety definition

Cambridge Dictionary

Retrieved from http://dictionary.cambridge.org

Chapter 2: Obsessive Compulsive Disorder

1. Obsessive Compulsive Disorder definition

Psychology Today website

Retrieved from http://www.psychologytoday.com/conditions/obsessive-compulsive-disorder

2. Pure Obsessional OCD definition

OCD Center of Los Angeles website

Retrieved from https://ocdla.com/obsessionalocd

Chapter 4: Triggers

1. "The most common triggers in BPD are related to relationships"

Kristalyn Salters-Pedneault (2017). *Understanding Borderline Personality Disorder Triggers.*

Retrieved from https://www.verywell.com/bpd-triggers-425475

Chapter 5: Fear of abandonment

1. Fear of abandonment

Jeffrey E. Young and Janet S. Klosko. (1994). *Reinventing Your Life.* Penguin Group: USA.

Chapter 6: Codependence

1. Codependence definition

Darlene Lancer. *Symptoms of Codependency.*

Retrieved from http://psychcentral.com/lib/symptoms-of-codependency/

Chapter 7: Emotional deprivation

1. Emotional deprivation lifetrap

Jeffrey E. Young and Janet S. Klosko. (1994). *Reinventing Your Life*. Penguin Group: USA.

Chapter 9: Addiction

1. Addiction definition

Psychology Today website

Retrieved from http://www.psychologytoday.com/basics/addiction

2. "The relationship between addiction and BPD has been described as a volatile one. Addictions are common in people who have BPD because they provide a way of distracting and numbing the pain from difficult emotions."

Borderline Personality Disorder and Addiction

Retrieved from http://www.dualdiagnosis.org/borderline-personality-disorder-and-addiction

Chapter 10: Unrelenting standards

1. Unrelenting standards lifetrap

Jeffrey E. Young and Janet S. Klosko. (1994). *Reinventing Your Life*. Penguin Group: USA.

Chapter 11: Mindfulness

1. "Mindfulness is the basic human ability to be fully present, aware of where we are and what we are doing, and not overly reactive or overwhelmed by what is going on around us."

Mindful website

Retrieved from https://www.mindful.org/what-is-mindfulness/

2. Benefits and brain changes with mindfulness meditation

Alice G. Walton. (2015). *7 Ways Meditation Can Actually Change the Brain.*

Retrieved from https://www.forbes.com/sites/alicegwalton/2015/02/09/7-ways-meditation-can-actually-change-the-brain/amp/

3. "Eventually, inspired by a moment in 'Eat Pray Love' where Elizabeth Gilbert had success with meditation and ended up meditating all night long, I decided that I would increase my meditation time – to a less impressive but still beneficial 15 minutes."

Elizabeth Gilbert. (2007). *Eat, Pray, Love: One Woman's Search For Everything Across Italy, India, and Indonesia.* Penguin Group: New York.

Chapter 12: Shame

1. "Author and research professor, Brene' Brown, who studies courage, vulnerability, shame and empathy, discusses that talking about our experiences sends shame out of hiding."

Brene Brown. (2008). *I Thought It Was Just Me (but it isn't): Telling the truth about perfectionism, inadequacy, and power.* Gotham Books: New York.

Chapter 13: Grace

1. "I first heard the word Grace when I was in my 20's and read the book, 'What's so Amazing about Grace?' by Phillip Yancey."

Phillip Yancey. (1997). *What's So Amazing About Grace?*

* Information was retrieved from websites in September 2017

About The Author

Monica Ashtyn Agius is from the beachside suburb of Umina Beach in Australia. Monica is passionate about mental health and the impact mental illness has on individuals, families and the wider community. In her first work of fiction Monica creates an authentic character who gives hope that recovery from mental illness is possible.

Printed in the United States
By Bookmasters